Revenge Is More Sweet
Than Bitter

Shannon Dunn

Revenge Is More Sweet Than Bitter

ISBN 978-0-9893763-1-0

This book is dedicated to my driving force and the center of my being, my husband, Shalom Dunn.

Chapter 1

J ayson had five more minutes to walk his two-timing, low down, snake in the grass behind through the double doors of our 4,000 square foot semi-mansion before his clothes went up in flames. I had already dragged over half of his wardrobe down the stairs where they sat in a pile in the middle of the foyer. His favorite genuine leather Versace's lay amid the heap; he had always bragged about how those damn shoes made the ladies do a double-take. That's exactly why I made sure to finish my masterpiece by placing them directly on top. They were like the cherry on an ice cream sundae – the final touch.

I sat on the bottom step with a lighter in one hand and our marriage certificate in the other, ready to do a reenactment of the infamous scene from *Waiting to Exhale*. I was a one-lady show and all I needed was my one-man audience. This time, there was absolutely no way I would let Jayson sweet talk his way out of trouble. Undoubtedly, Jayson was a smooth talker. It was a trait that made him one of the top defense attorneys in Las Vegas. His creamy, caramel complexion, hypnotizing, big, round eyes and that irresistible dimple in his chin made him nothing short of the finest specimen I had ever laid eyes on, but it was his captivating and charming personality that had me hooked from day one. Five years ago when I had found myself in a bit of trouble with the law, my mother had called on him to represent me. He was the son of one of her old schoolmates that owed her a big favor. Jayson was able to get my case dismissed and a love affair quickly blossomed. Not only had he saved my ass from going to prison, but he moved me out of my mother's house, which enabled me to finally escape her suffocating control – something I had dreamed of doing for years. I loved Jayson and owed him a lot, however, that didn't mean I had to continue accepting his dumb-ass excuses for all his bullshit, like the unexplained numbers in his cell phone, the scent of perfume on his clothes and his coming home at all times of the night.

It was 2:55 a.m. and somehow, Jayson had not managed to find his way home or to a phone to call me. His late night rendezvous weren't unusual. It usually happened a couple of times a week and was followed by the excuse that he stayed late at the office, poring over documents for some important case. I stopped believing that excuse after we had been married for a year and he came home reeking of some bitch's cheap gardenia body spray. He had sworn up and down that the smell had come from an air freshener that his secretary had sprayed in his office. The following morning, a beautiful pair of three caret diamond earrings and a bouquet of white roses were delivered to my doorstep by carrier. The card read, *May our love stand as strong as a fortress: impenetrable, a haven for our souls to exist together and for always.*

Love, Your husband, Jayson.

That's Jayson: romantic, charismatic and always finding his way out of a jam. Even though I pretended like everything was okay after the perfume incident, I never really trusted him again. I started paying closer attention to things. I began checking his pants pockets and cell phone when he wasn't looking. I even checked his boxers for unusual stains when I did laundry. I refused to be blindsided like some of those women I'd heard of - the kind of women who ignore all the clues and don't believe their husbands are cheating until they walk into their bedroom and see him with some ditzy blonde spread eagle on top of their brand new down comforter. I was not going to be *that* woman. Jayson was beginning to overstep his boundaries and tonight, I planned on getting "my house" back under control. Maybe the two bottles of Merlot I had downed while waiting up for him and watching two episodes of Cheaters had me a little tipsy, but I was fully aware of what I was about to do.

I heard the jingle of his key in the front lock and looked at the clock; it read 2:58 a.m. Lucky for him - two more minutes and he would have walked into a nice, warm bonfire. As soon as I saw his face, my body started to tingle and my heart started to melt. I gathered my wits, stood up and looked him dead in the eye. Jayson only glanced at me briefly before gawking at the mess on the floor and closing the door behind him.

"Genevieve, what the hell is going on?" Jayson asked, his face twisted in confusion.

"Don't I need to be asking you that question? It's almost three in the morning and you strut in here like your shit doesn't stink and like there's absolutely nothing wrong with a married man coming home odd hours of the night."

"I told you before, it's part of my job," he responded.

"I don't want to hear your tired excuses anymore. You could have called me and told me you were going to be late."

"I'm sorry, baby, I just got caught up in my work and lost track of time. But this is uncalled for," he said, pointing to the heap of clothes on the floor.

"You don't tell me what's fucking uncalled for," I screamed, waving our marriage certificate in the air then raising the lighter up to the edge of it.

"Genevieve, have you lost your mind? I'm calling Mama Rose right now. Maybe she can talk some sense into you," he said, walking into the living room to find the telephone. I was quickly on his heels with my pink, silk robe flapping behind me.

"You will do no such thing. I am a grown-ass woman! Our affairs are none of my mother's business," I yelled. It pissed me off that he was threatening to call my mother on me like I was a child. He knew damn well that I resented the control that Mama Rose had over me for so many years. She had tried to dictate almost every part of my life up until I married him when I was twenty-six years old. I loved my mother dearly, but she no longer had any say-so in my personal matters.

"You know you're not accustomed to drinking and you drank two bottles of wine. No wonder you're acting nuts," he said, picking up the two empty Merlot bottles off the coffee table and tossing them in the garbage can.

"I'm not drunk and I know exactly what I'm doing. I'm burning our marriage certificate since you don't respect our vows anymore and then, I'm going to burn all your clothes just for the fun of it," I stated with certainty and a wry smirk.

Jayson turned around and grabbed me by the wrist. I looked in his eyes and expected to see anger, but instead, his eyes were soft and pleading.

"Genevieve, when I first met you, I knew you were spirited, feisty and, quite frankly, a handful, but that's exactly what I liked about you. You are sure of yourself and have strong conviction in what you believe in, but this time, what you believe to be fact is fiction. I would never cheat on you. You are everything I want in a woman. Smart, beautiful, sexy… another woman could never fill your shoes."

Jayson wrapped his arms around me. I lay my head against his chest. His heartbeat sang in my ear. I had given in once again. There would be no bonfire tonight, other than the fire we would make in the bedroom.

"Besides, I know if I cheated, you would kill me!" Jayson said, laughing.

I laughed along with him, but felt coldness in my heart - a coldness that even chilled me. Would he ever know how close he really was to the truth?

Chapter 2

Lunch with your mother on a Sunday should be a pleasant excursion, full of female chatter, giggles and girly advice, but Mama Rose had a way of turning a tea for two into nuclear warfare in a matter of minutes. We had barely sat down and looked at our menus before she started.

"Mm, mm, mmm, now that's a damn shame that they done gone and gave all these perfectly good white and colored folks jobs to these illegals," she said, referring to the Hispanic waiter that had just seated us. She shook her napkin out and placed it neatly on her lap. It was bizarre how she could act so prim and proper while speaking so offensively.

"First off, we are not colored people anymore, Mama Rose. We are African-Americans and you really should not stereotype people. How do you know that our waiter is an illegal? And by the way, there are illegal aliens and immigrants in America of many different nationalities. They don't just come from Hispanic countries," I stated as calmly as I could to avoid offending her.

"Don't sass me, girl! I ain't no fool and I ain't raise no fool. You know these Mexicans is overpopulating and taking over America. I may not have no fancy-smancy degree like you, but I don't need one to know that our country is being turned into Tijuana. Now, sit up straight and stop slouching like a lumberjack," she fussed.

If I could have gotten up and walked out right then, I would have. Doing so would only have caused her to make a louder scene. It was my fault for agreeing to go out to lunch with her in the first place. Jayson and I normally spent our Sundays lounging around the house, watching old westerns or the cooking channel. We usually slept in, ordered out and on some Sundays, we didn't even change out of our pajamas or comb our hair. Sundays were our day to relax together, but today he had gotten called into work. When Mama Rose called and suggested we go out to lunch, I was feeling lonely and depressed, which was the only reason I even agreed to go.

Romano's was an Italian restaurant with good food and great service. Jayson and I frequented it often, so I hoped Mama Rose would not embarrass me enough to make me not want to come back.

"Oh, my! Isn't that Deacon Jameson from my church sitting at that table in the corner?" Mama Rose asked me, focusing her attention to a couple on the other side of the room.

"How would I know? I've only been to your church once and I don't remember a Deacon Jameson," I replied.

I glanced over at the table Mama Rose was peering at. An older gentleman in a conservative suit and tie was sitting across from a lady much younger than himself. She had on a form-fitting short red skirt and red pumps to match. If the neckline of her blouse went down any further, her breasts were likely to fall out right into her bowl of soup.

I didn't remember either of their faces from the hundreds of people Mama Rose had introduced me to when I had visited Holy Trust Baptist Church with her over a year ago.

"Well, I ain't blind. I know who Deacon Jameson is 'cause I go to church every Sunday, unlike some folks," she said, looking at me and sucking her teeth. "And that there is not Mrs. Jameson and it ain't his daughter, Kimberly, either. Hell, Kimberly big as a whale, she couldn't fit in that hoe skirt that young hussy got on if she wanted to. I have a mind to go tell his sinnin', two-timin' ass off right now. To think he was in church this morning, preaching the gospel and no more than two hours later, he sitting here sinnin'. I wish the Lord would strike him dead right now!"

Mama Rose closed her eyes as if in prayer for Deacon Jameson to croak at this exact moment. Mama Rose concentrated so hard on her prayer that I looked over at their table again to make sure Deacon Jameson hadn't actually passed on and fallen into his plate of linguini.

"Men are no-good, dirty dogs and they need to be kept on short leashes. Your father was no good, too, but that's another story. You need to keep your eyes on that husband of yours. He's nice-looking, rolling in money and he ain't never at home. If you don't watch it, some other lady is gonna snatch your man right up from under your nose," Mama Rose said, as she casually scanned over the menu.

She had hit a sore spot with me, as she was so skillful at doing. I needed an immediate break from her before I lost my mind.

"Excuse me. I need to go to the ladies' room," I said, already getting up from the table and heading to the rear of the restaurant.

The pressure in my head deflated as soon as I left Mama Rose's presence. In the restroom, I splashed a handful of cool water in my face and stared at my reflection in the mirror. Although I had just turned thirty, I barely looked over the age of twenty. Whenever Jayson and I went out for drinks, I still always got asked for my identification. My features were appealing: high cheekbones, blemish-free, almond-colored skin, piercing, dark brown eyes and thick, curly, shoulder-length hair. I was very particular about how I dressed and would not be caught dead without a sexy pair of heels on. I couldn't imagine what Jayson would want with another woman, but then again, there are men who would have sex with a one-legged, hunch-backed, denture-wearing tranny if they thought no one would find out. I hoped my suspicions about him cheating were just a figment of my elaborate imagination - both for his sake and mine.

By the time I returned to the table, the Deacon and his mistress had left the restaurant. I breathed a sigh of relief, hoping their departure would calm Mama Rose down somewhat.

"Girl, you took so damn long in the restroom that I went ahead and ordered for you. I got you the chef salad with no eggs, no dressing and no croutons. You've been looking a little wide in the hips lately, so I figured I'd help you cut some calories," Mama Rose said as I sat down. And she said it all with a genuine smile. She truly believed she had done me a favor by ordering me a lunch fit for a rabbit. She paused, as if waiting for a thank you. I didn't respond. Instead, I pretended to enjoy the driest salad I had ever had in my life. Out of the corner of my eye, I saw Mama Rose roll her eyes at me. I didn't care. There was no way I was going to thank her for the lettuce and carrots she had ordered for me when my mouth had been watering for Romano's signature spaghetti and meatballs. Now, I couldn't wait to leave Romano's and I also couldn't wait until Jayson got home. I knew when I picked up the phone this morning and heard Bret's voice on the other end that it meant our Sunday was ruined. Bret was Jayson's best friend and co-worker. They were both top attorneys at Franklin and Franklin Law Firm. I had become accustomed to Bret calling or stopping by the house on the weekend, but a phone call from him at 7 in the morning could only mean one thing: they needed Jayson in the office. I glanced at my watch. It was still early. If he got home by 5 p.m., we still had time to order Chinese and catch a horror flick on television.

"You in a rush or something?" Mama Rose asked after she caught me checking my watch several times.

"No, Mama Rose. I'm just a little anxious for Jayson to get home from work. We had planned on spending the day together."

"Like I said earlier, you need to watch him. He ain't never at home. That only means one thing in my book."

"Jayson has a very demanding job. I knew that when I married him. There's no reason for me to get upset or to be jumping to conclusions just because he has been putting in a lot of extra hours lately," I stated defensively and in part, trying desperately to convince myself that my words held truth.

"Well, that's a load of rubbish! If telling yourself that makes you sleep better at night, then you keep right on lying to yourself. Jayson may be uppity and educated, but he like him some poontang the same as any other man. And I'm sure the size, shape or color don't much matter to him, as long as it's warm."

I almost choked on my romaine lettuce. I looked around the room to make sure no one nearby overheard Mama Rose's vulgar comment.

Her behavior still embarrassed me, although she had spoken this way for as long as I could remember.

Mama Rose was a southern woman to the heart. She was born and raised in Memphis, could gut a pig in 30 seconds and fix the best meal you ever had in 10 minutes. She didn't take mess from anyone and had raised me and my sister, Georgette, to be as straight-forward and to the point as she was. Mama Rose had tried to control every detail of me and my sister's lives, from the way we ate and dressed to the people we dated, from the time we were born until well into our adulthood. My older sister, Georgette, had long ago moved far-away to escape Mama Rose's firm grasp. She lived across the country in Panama City, Florida, where Mama Rose could only reach her by phone. She was the smart one. On the other hand, I had taken Mama Rose's advice to go an in-state college and stay at home under her reign until I graduated. Since I ended up pursuing a Master's Degree in Psychology, I was still living under her roof when I had found myself in a bit of trouble and was introduced to Jayson. The fact that he had helped me escape Mama Rose's rule was enough to call him my Prince Charming. The fact that he bought me anything I asked for, took me on extravagant vacations regularly and could make me holler in the bedroom was all an added bonus.

Mama Rose liked Jayson, but he fell into a category of persons that she held an enormous disdain for: **men**. I don't remember my father that much since he died when I was only eight years old, but I believed she held the same distrust and contempt for him as she did for all other men. She never talked about him that much after he died unless she was referring to him as a lying dog, a conniving motherfucker or in some other negative reference.

I would be ever grateful to Jayson for the simple fact that I no longer had to wake up to Mama Rose's un-objective negativity. Jayson was one of the best things that ever happened to me. I wanted to have children with him one day. I wanted us to grow old and gray together. That's why I hated to admit that my mother was right about one thing: Jayson was spending way too much time away from the house. I would just have to try harder to make our time together special. After last night, I wanted things between me and Jayson to change.

While Mama Rose buzzed away about how inappropriately the first lady of her church dressed, I drowned her out and began to plan a new start for me and Jayson. I decided to try my best to stop accusing him of cheating and to spice things up. I would start tonight. When he got home from work, I planned on surprising him at the door with a pink and white teddy that I had tucked away in my dresser with the tag still on it. Instead of the usual Chinese take-out, I would cook a nice meal - something that I hated to do. We could have a nice candle-light dinner by the fireplace and I could be his dessert. I got excited just thinking about it.

"Girl, are you even listening to me?" Mama Rose snapped.

"Yeah, Mama Rose, I'm listening. You said the first lady of your church dresses like a whore and you wish the Lord would strike her dead... just the usual."

Chapter 3

After lunch with Mama Rose, I rushed home to start getting things in order for me and Jayson's special night. Tonight would be the start of a new beginning for us. As soon as I stepped out of the shower, the phone rang. My best friend, Myeisha, was on the other end. I had barely finished saying "hello" before she started talking.

"I have been trying to call you all afternoon. You haven't been answering your house phone or your cell phone," Myeisha ranted. "Are you and Jayson over there getting it on or something?"

"Can I get a 'hello' or 'how are you doing' before you start going off?" I asked Myeisha with an exaggerated sigh.

"Bitch, you know I ain't down for all that formal shit. So, are you and Jayson busy fucking or what?"

Myeisha was the only person in the world who could get away with calling me bitch without getting cursed out or worse. We had known each other ever since my mother, Georgette and I had moved to Las Vegas when I was twelve years old. We went through adolescence together and were so close that we even had our first periods on the same day. She was hard as a rock on the outside, but on the inside, she was very sensitive and fragile, just like me. We shared the same interests, like traveling, collecting rare coins and a good scary movie. I felt closer to her than I did to my own biological sister. We were inseparable. She was the only one that I shared intimate details of me and Jayson's relationship with. I trusted her with everything, including most of my deepest and darkest secrets.

"Jayson got called into work today, so I went out to lunch with Mama Rose, which, of course, was a huge mistake. My phone was turned off because you know how pissed Mama Rose gets if I'm on the phone when I'm supposed to be spending time with her."

"Glad to hear Mama Rose is doing alright. I know if she is still giving you the blues, she couldn't be doing any better," Myeisha laughed. She loved Mama Rose just as much as I did, but she also knew how trying my mother could be.

"Can you believe she will be sixty this year and still curses like a sailor, although she claims she is "saved" and professes to be a shepherd for the Lord? Today, she accused the deacon at her church of having an affair and the pastor's wife of dressing like a whore."

"Speaking of whores," Myeisha began with excitement in her voice. "The Galaxy Club is having an all-male review tonight. There will be nothing but sexy hunks of chocolate on the stage, shaking what their mamas gave them, all night long. Locals get in free up until midnight and I'm not taking any excuses from you, so I'll pick you up at ten."

"Wow, I didn't know the freaks come out on Sunday nights, too," I joked. "I mean, really, what happened to a day for rest and worship?"

"This is Vegas, baby. We do worship. We just worship hot bods and casino chips."

"Well, sorry, but I already have plans with Jayson tonight. Plus, you know I'm a married woman. Strip clubs really aren't my thing."

"You don't have to remind me that you're married. Remember, I was the maid of honor at your wedding. You know that I would never try to tarnish you and Jayson's relationship *if* I thought he was doing right by you, but the key word here is 'if'. Take my advice: Jayson is a wannabe player and you should show him that two can play that game."

I took Myeisha's advice on a lot of things, but relationships were not one of them. At thirty, she had already been divorced twice. Her first marriage, to a police officer, ended when she beat him up after finding incriminating e-mails from another woman to him. She had taken a baseball bat and clobbered him with it so severely that when I went to visit him in the hospital I couldn't even recognize him. Luckily for her, he was so embarrassed about being assaulted by a 110 lb. woman, he made up some story about being in a horrible bike accident instead of pressing charges.

Her second marriage to a gentleman twenty years her senior had only lasted 18 months before she got bored and began to cheat on him. Even when he found out she had been cheating, he still wanted to work things out with her, but Myeisha continued to sabotage their relationship simply because being monogamous was way too boring for her.

A Halle Berry look-a-like, Myeisha could get any man that she wanted, and she did. She was a bit promiscuous, to say the least. She frequented strip clubs, always juggled at least three boyfriends at a time and had even experimented with other women. And I wasn't about to let Myeisha drag me into her craziness.

"I don't have any real proof that Jayson is cheating and until I do, I am not willing to risk ruining our relationship. The perfume on his clothes and him coming home late is not hard evidence that he is actually cheating. In a court of law, they would call that circumstantial evidence. It's not enough to prove guilt," I stated.

"Drop the courtroom antics, Genevieve. Perfume on his clothes is pretty hard evidence. In the street, we don't call it circumstantial; we call it cold busted. Really, Genevieve, I can't believe you are being so naïve and blind. Husband or not, I've never known you to take any shit from anyone, besides me and Mama Rose. Are you getting soft?"

Myeisha was right. I had let Jayson cross a line, but there was nothing more I wanted in this world than for my marriage to work.

"Look, you're on your own tonight. Like I said, me and Jayson have plans tonight that I am not about to break just so some stranger can swing his nasty manhood in my face," I said loudly and clearly into the phone to make sure Myeisha got the message.

"Fine, have it your way. Be a faithful wife to your cheating husband. Shoot, he's probably at the strip club right now. Work!? Yeah, right! The only thing he's working on is sticking a hundred dollar bill in some broad's G-string."

"Myeisha, I just got out the shower and I haven't dried off. I'll call you tomorrow and you can update me on your latest sexual encounter that I'm sure you will have with some random man or woman tonight."

Mama Rose and Myeisha may have been convinced that Jayson was creeping around, but I wasn't and until I had some hard evidence I wasn't about to give up on my man that easily.

"Okay, but call me if you need me to whip his ass. I know some brothers who will do it for the price of a Happy Meal and a couple of forty ounces," Myeisha giggled.

I loved Myeisha, but I was more than happy to end our call. Maybe what I needed was for everyone to get out of our business so I could concentrate on taking care of Jayson's needs. I dried off, applied my favorite lavender-scented lotion and laid my pink and white teddy out on the bed. Jayson had given it to me for a Valentine's Day gift last year and it still had not been worn. I would slip into it after I prepared us a nice dinner. I had two hours to put something together. Hopefully, that would be enough time to complete a full course meal, even if I burned something and had to start over, like I usually did. I threw on a robe and headed downstairs, ready to prepare my man the best meal he ever had.

After an hour and a half of cooking and thirty minutes of cleaning up the colossal mess I had made in the kitchen, I felt sweaty, hot and in need of another shower. It was 5:00 pm and I was expecting Jayson home at any moment. I frantically ran upstairs and jumped back in the shower. I wanted tonight to be absolutely perfect. Despite the mess I had made, the pasta, lobster tails and tossed salad had turned out pretty good. I had even baked a pie (Sara Lee straight out of the box, of course).

By the time I had finished taking a quick shower, putting on my teddy and pinning my hair up in a bun, allowing several ringlets to fall down and frame my face, it was 6:00 pm - a whole hour after the time I had expected Jayson to be home. I tried his cell phone, but only got his voicemail. After the third attempt to contact him, I could feel my blood beginning to boil. What if he didn't come home until the wee of hours of the morning, like he had so many other times before? I tried to not be so pessimistic. After all, I had wanted a new start and that meant I needed to have a new attitude about things. I tried to look at things more objectively. Maybe he was tied up in traffic or working on some murder case that required all his attention. If so, why wouldn't he just call and tell me he would be late. I could accept that he had a very demanding career, one that required him to work flexible hours and to be called away unexpectedly. What I couldn't accept was that he could not find the decency to pick up a phone to let me know that he would be a little late.

Just as I had decided to throw on a robe and call it a day, I heard a car pull into the driveway. The pebbles on the street crunched under the weight of the vehicle, alerting me to Jayson's arrival. A smile spread across my face. He hadn't let me down after all. This was proof in the pudding; he wanted things to work just as much as I did. I tore off the robe, revealing my lingerie and ran into the closet to slip on a pair of heels. I glanced over my shoulder at my reflection in the mirror one last time before heading downstairs. I liked what I saw. My soft ringlets and natural make-up made my face look innocent and angelic, but my 3-inch heels and barely-there teddy said va, va, vroom, as it hugged my sumptuous curves in all the right places. Jayson's late arrival meant that I would have to reheat the food, but the night was far from ruined. I rushed down the stairs to meet him. I heard his footsteps coming up the walkway and before he could stick his key in the lock, I swung the door open, leaning against the doorframe in my sex-iest pose and purred "surprise" in my most sensual Marilyn Monroe voice.

Only the surprise was on me when it wasn't Jayson's big, round eyes that stared back at me. Instead, Bret's blue eyes gazed upon me so intensely that I could feel my skin burning. He slowly looked up and down my body, studying every inch of my anatomy. His eyes fi-nally rested on my breasts and his lips curled up into a wide, devilish grin. It took me a moment to get past the shock enough to respond. I pushed the door nearly closed, leaving only a crack and hid my ex-posed body behind its solid mahogany wood.

"I'm sorry, I didn't mean to intrude, but Jayson sent me over," Bret stated. His grin had disappeared and he looked genuinely apologetic.

"Stay here, I'll be right back," I said, closing the door and leaving him on the porch. I ran upstairs, slipped into my robe and exchanged my heels for a pair of furry, red house slippers. When I opened the door, Bret was still standing there, tapping his feet and whistling a tune. He acted surprised to see me, like the incident moments before had never happened.

"Come in," I said, blushing. I knew it would be a while before I could look at Bret without thinking about what had just happened, but for now, I would have to get over the embarrassment if I wanted to know why he was at the door instead of Jayson.

I could read Bret's expression as I lead him to the living room. Half burned candles that I had strategically placed around the living and dining room for ambiance flickered as wax built up at their bottoms. A blanket lay in front of the crackling fireplace and the dinner that I had painstakingly prepared sat untouched on our marble table. Bret took in his surroundings. He looked uncomfortable and I don't think it had anything to do with him seeing me nearly naked. Something was weighing heavily on his mind.

"Have a seat," I said, pointing to a leather sectional. Bret sat down and started fidgeting with a crystal candy dish on the coffee table. It had been a gift from Mama Rose for our wedding. Jayson always ate the butterscotch candies that I put in them when he sat there and watched television, so it was empty, but Bret concentrated on the dish like it was the most interesting thing he had ever seen. There was no mistaking from the tense expression on Bret's face that I wasn't going to like whatever it was he was here to tell me.

I really liked Bret. He was a good friend to both me and Jayson. He had helped Jayson find the house we were living in. For our wedding, he had even given us the full down payment on it as a gift. He didn't have a family of his own, although he was a nice-looking man. Myeisha always said that if she ever decided to date white men, he would be the first one on her list. Jayson and Bret had worked together at Franklin and Franklin long before Jayson had met me. They planned to open their own firm together one day. They were almost as inseparable as me and Myeisha.

"So, where's Jayson?" I questioned, cutting straight to the chase.

"He's still tied up at work. We are working on a really important case. Our client is facing life in prison for murder. We know he's innocent, but the prosecuting team has managed to manufacture some really hard and convincing evidence against him. We working our butts off to try to save this guy's hide."

Bret declared this as if everything would all make sense to me now. I gave him a cynical look, then sat on the edge of an ottoman directly across from him. I wasn't in the mood for any games, which was exactly what he was playing with me.

"Bret, I know that you and Jayson are like brothers. Your loyalty lies with him. But, please do not come into my house and disrespect me by lying to me like I'm some fool. If you are both working on the case, then why are you here and not him?"

"You are my friend, too, Genevieve," Bret stated. He looked me in the eyes, but only for a moment before looking down at his hands. "Jayson is the senior attorney on the case. I'm just assisting him, so my input is not always required, but his is crucial."

"So, you mean to tell me I'm supposed to believe that he can't break away for a second to call his wife and let me know he's alive and safe?" I asked.

"He's interviewing our client in jail. They won't allow cell phones inside. He knew you would be upset. That's why he had me come personally to let you know that he would be home around eight."

"Eight o'clock, huh?" I murmured, with doubt. I didn't know if Bret knew about my short stay in jail years ago. Knowing how hard Jayson tried to keep up with appearances, he probably had not told Bret, or anyone else for that matter, that he'd met his wife while she was an inmate in the city jail. The last time I was there, visiting hours ended promptly at five o'clock - no exceptions, not even for hot stuff attorneys.

"You know, I really hate that Jayson is putting you in the middle of his web of lies. I wouldn't want you to get trapped in it. That could be real dangerous," I said, walking over to the bar.

I poured myself a glass of wine. There was a time when I would not touch alcohol, but it had become my friend lately. It replaced the loneliness I felt whenever Jayson was not around. I offered Bret a drink, but he declined. He looked uneasy and ready to leave. I started walking to the front door, offering him a chance to escape. He nearly tripped over himself as he jumped up from the couch to follow me. I held the door open for him, permitting his exit. His warm breath on the back of my neck startled me as he came up from behind, allowing his chest to brush up against my back.

"I'm sorry, Geneieve. Call me if you need *anything*," he whispered into my ear from behind.

He brushed passed me and walked out into the darkness. It took me a while to figure out if the chill bumps on my skin had come from the cool night breeze or Bret's soft lips next to my ears.

Chapter 4

I was supposed to meet Myeisha in 10 minutes at the Boulevard Mall. I was looking forward to getting out of the house. A shopping excursion was just the distraction I needed to take my mind off of everything that was going on. I sped down Interstate 15 and exited on the off-ramp to the mall. The sun was out, but a few scattered clouds threatened rain. If the rain could wash away my foul mood that would be great, but I knew the clouds were teasing me, suggesting something they were not willing to provide. It was kind of like me and Jayson's relationship. He more than suggested, but actually swore in front of hundreds on our wedding day to love, honor and cherish me. He had told me that I was all he had ever wanted and all he ever needed. Now, I couldn't get the sorry son-of-a bitch to come home for dinner.

When Jayson had finally come home at 8:30 last night, I pretended to be asleep. He nudged me a few times. I groaned and mumbled incoherently so he would think I was in a deep sleep. He eventually climbed into bed, wrapped his arm around me and was snoring minutes later. When I was sure that he was fast asleep, I lifted his arm from around my waist and scooted as near to the edge of the bed as I could without falling off. I didn't want the mistake of his skin touching mine. When I woke up this morning, he had already left for work. I found a note on the pillow apologizing and promising to make things up to me tonight. As I was heading out of the door to meet Myeisha, a deliverer arrived with the standard dozen, white roses that Jayson always sent when he was trying to make up for a wrong. I didn't take the time to admire their scent like I normally did. This time, I just sat them on the floor by the door and went on my way.

I spotted Myeisha in the food court at Pretzel Time. She looked like a teenager from behind. She sported a pair of dark blue skinny jeans, a bright pink tank top and was carrying a solid gold purse bigger than she was. She was so engrossed in flirting with the cashier that she didn't even see me approaching. I tapped her on her shoulder to get her attention.

"Can you wait a freakin' minute!" she said, turning around ready to swing on someone. "Oh my gosh, Gen! I'm sorry. I didn't know you were standing behind me!" she explained, giving me a hug.

"And I didn't know you were into teenage boys barely getting paid minimum wage," I replied.

"It's all in good fun," she stated, winking at the cashier as she paid for her order. He flashed her a wide grin. I could tell by the way he was staring at her that he wanted to have fun and so much more. Myeisha thought it was amusing to flaunt her beauty and alluring energy at people and then walk away. She didn't understand that desire could be deadly, that if someone wanted something bad enough, they might be willing to take it.

"Myeisha, you're going to attract the worst kind of trouble one day, like a stalker or worse," I warned.

"And you going to give yourself a headache worrying about me," she replied. "By the way, you look like you could use some Tylenol and a shot of vodka right now."

"Yeah, well, things didn't turn out quite as planned last night," I mumbled. I didn't want to hear her say "I told you so," but she had been right. Jayson had left me hanging.

The food court was on the second floor and overlooked the main entrance of the mall. I studied the couples as they entered. It was easy to guess if they were still dating or already married. It was pretty obvious that the couples that tugged screaming kids along were married. The married men held haggard expressions of confusion on their face, they were almost never holding their significant others' hands and some of them even had the nerve to walk 5 feet in front of their wives while she lagged behind, struggling with the children. The couples that I assumed were still in the dating phase of their relationship were holding onto each other so closely, it was as if they thought someone might come along and kidnap their loved one at any given moment. Only a year ago, Jayson and I would have blended in well with them, holding onto each other for our dear lives.

"Earth to Genevieve," Myeisha said, snapping her well-manicured fingers in front of my face. "So, are you going to tell me what happened?"

"Yeah, I'm sorry. I just have a lot on my mind," I whispered, snapping back into reality.

"Look, Gen," Myeisha said, reaching across the table and taking my hand in hers. "I can tell that you're in pain. As much as I wouldn't mind if you kicked Jayson's sorry-ass to the curb, I know that you love him and your heart is breaking. Maybe he really isn't cheating, Gen. Maybe there's an explanation for all of this."

"No, you were right. He's never there and even when he is, he isn't. Myeisha, I don't know what to do. I think my marriage is falling apart," I cried, allowing my tears to flow for the first time.

Myeisha handed me a napkin. The busy crowd around us continued to stuff their mouths with high fat, high carb food, totally oblivious to my sorrows.

"I need to know. I need to know if Jayson is cheating on me," I moaned.

"Well, let's find out," Myeisha said. Her eyes sparkled and I could tell she had come up with a plan.

Chapter 5

"And how do you suppose we are going to find out if Jayson is really cheating? He already has Bret covering for him," I said.

"Of course he does. Dogs always cover each other's tracks," Myeisha stated, sucking her teeth. "That's why we need to throw him a bone and see if he knows how to fetch."

I wondered exactly what Myeisha had up her sleeve. At this point, I was willing to try anything to find out what Jayson was up to.

"I say we send in a decoy," she said. "Some cute little thing with a big butt, even bigger breasts and a cute smile."

"You mean, set him up," I said, shaking my head in disagreement.

"You're acting like we are forcing him do something. We aren't making him do anything. If he's a dog, he'll go for the bone and if he's not, well then, you have nothing to worry about."

I didn't like the idea of sending some woman after my man. But, Myeisha was right. If Jayson was a loyal, committed husband like he claimed to be, then I should have nothing to worry about.

"Okay, if I agree to your crazy shenanigan, who will be the decoy?"

"Do you remember my homegirl, Candance?"

I had met several of Myeisha's friends and co-workers, but her name didn't ring a bell. I shook my head no.

"Before she started to work at the bank with me, she stripped at China Dolls. She has a killer body and she's intelligent enough to hold her own with Jayson. Plus, you don't have to worry about her falling for none of his smooth-talking because she is already engaged to be married this summer."

I still did not remember who Candance was, but I trusted Myeisha's judgment.

"Do you think we should pay her to approach him?" I asked, unsure of how things like this worked.

"I told you she's my homegirl. She'll do it for free. Her last boyfriend cheated on her and with her own sister, at that. I'm sure she will be more than happy to help us out."

My stomach churned. Maybe it was because I had been too upset to eat anything all day or maybe it was because I was agreeing to send some stripper gallivanting after my husband. I could not believe that our relationship had come to this. All I wanted was for Jayson to be the faithful husband that he had promised to be.

Before we had even left the food court, our plan was already underway. Myeisha immediately called Candance with the proposition. Just like Myeisha had said, Candance was more than happy to assist us in busting Jayson. Since I knew Jayson always hung out on Friday nights at Posh, a local upscale lounge, it was easy to set up the date, time and location. There was no doubt that he would be there. It was a ritual that he and the other male attorneys at Franklin and Franklin practiced religiously. I gave Myeisha a wedding picture from my wallet for Candance to identify Jayson by. My hand was shaking as I handed it to her.

"Girl, calm down," Myeisha said. "Think about it this way. By the end of Friday night, you'll know if Jayson's worth keeping or if you should throw him back in the pond with all the other guppies."

Although I craved the truth, I feared what would happen if I found out he was a deceitful scumbag.

Myeisha could feel my anxiety, so for the rest of the afternoon, we both tried to avoid the subject. We mostly window shopped. Myeisha went into a few stores, but only made one purchase - a pair of three inch silver heels. I wasn't feeling up to shopping today, which was odd since spending money usually made me feel better. I knew I was in a deep funk that I had to get out of. The only thing that could make me feel better was finding out if Jayson was really cheating on me.

"You need to let loose and live a little, Genevieve," Myeisha said, observing my sour disposition. I'm sure *Jayson* isn't walking around moping."

I wished Myeisha would stop bringing him up; it was only making me feel worse.

"You never told me about how things went the other night. You know, at the strip club," I said, trying to shift topics.

"It was nothing but fine-ass brothers willing do anything for a dollar. How do you think it went?" Myeisha laughed.

"Being in strip club to you must be like being in Disneyland to a kid," I joked.

"Correction, you mean Disneyworld."

"I stand corrected," I giggled. Although Myeisha could be a little pushy, over the top and a nymphomaniac, she always knew how to make me laugh.

"There was this one stripper, Hot Chocolate. Girl, he was so fine that it brought tears to my eyes. I was tempted to bring him home with me," Myeisha declared.

"I'm surprised you didn't. I've seen you do worse. Like the time we were barbecuing at your house and you went to the grocery store for hamburger buns and came back with some guy named Tony. Me and your other guests ended up in the backyard eating hamburgers with no buns while you and Tony disappeared in your room for an hour."

"Yeah... Tony," Myeisha whispered, deep in thought. "I almost forgot about him. Tony didn't have anything on Hot Chocolate, but you can't actually bring a stripper home. That's definitely an unsaid rule."

"I didn't think you had any rules."

"I have lots of rules," Myeisha informed me. "For starters, never get emotionally involved or I'll end up like you - married and miserable. Never get involved with married men because they're controlling and I don't want to end up with a pissed –off, psychopathic wife on my hands. Never date anyone that looks better than me because then, I'm not the center of attention and never let someone in your house that you don't want drinking out of your cups. The last rule applies to strippers. I've seen what they do in those V.I.P. rooms at the strip clubs."

"I'm sure you have," I said, shooting Myeisha a knowing glare.

"Don't get mad at me because I like to have a little fun every now and then and you choose to sit around the house, waiting for Jayson's low-life ass to come home. Honestly, Genevieve, ever since you married Jayson, you act like you can't have fun anymore unless it involves him. I remember when you would be at the club right next to me, dancing and having fun. Now, you act like the word 'fun' could bring on the black plague."

Myeisha slowed her pace to check out some guy going through the pants rack in Big and Tall, a suit store for larger men who had problems finding clothes in regular stores. He was at least 6'5, with feet that looked like row boats - right up Myeisha's alley. He looked up and spotted Myeisha spying on him through the store's window and he flashed her a huge smile. Myeisha played the shy role by blushing and nervously running her fingers through her hair. Only *I* knew that Myeisha did not have a shy bone in her body. He handed the store clerk a pair of pants that he was holding and ran out to meet her. Up close, he looked even taller than he did in the store. Next to Myeisha's 5"2 frame, he looked like the Jolly Green Giant. Within minutes, they had exchanged phone numbers and arranged their first date. I had to give it to Myeisha: she could play men like a fiddle.

"His name doesn't ring a bell, but he looks familiar. I think he might be a basketball player," Myeisha whispered, as we walked away. "Sorry, I got a little distracted. Now, what were we talking about?"

"You were saying that I don't know have to have fun, which isn't true. I still know how to have fun. I just don't think the type of fun you like having is very appropriate for a married woman," I asserted.

"It's not like I'm asking you to break your vows and sleep with someone. I just asked you to go the strip club with me. You don't have to touch unless you want to," Myeisha said playfully nudging me. "Besides, I see plenty of women at the club with wedding rings on. Their husbands probably love it. Long Dong Juan gets their lady all fired up and then, she comes home hot and ready. What more could a husband ask for? Sex with the foreplay already out of the way."

"It's not the strip club that's bad, but the choices that people seem to make in them that leads to trouble," I advised.

"And since you aren't going to make any bad choices because you love your husband, then you shouldn't have any problems going with me tomorrow night," Myeisha coaxed.

Although she was convincing, there were other factors at play that had influenced me to give in. I wanted to find myself again. My identity had become so intertwined with being Jayson's wife that I felt lost. I needed to know that I could exist without him again, if fate had that in store. There was also a bruise on my ego that made me want to show Jayson that I did not have to sit around waiting for gifts of attention from him.

"So, you'll go?" Myeisha begged.

"Okay, okay, I'll go," I moaned.

Myeisha jumped up and down like a kid in a candy store. She had finally won the battle.

Chapter 6

Mama Rose's face at my door at six o'clock in the morning was not what I would call the start to a good day. It was more like waking up to a nightmare.

"What's going on," I said, as I opened the front door and rubbed sleep from my eyes with the back of my hand. She had been frantically ringing the doorbell. I had jumped up out of bed, slipped on one of Jayson's oversized t-shirts and made a mad dash to the front door in order to stop the incessant ringing. Now, my head was swimming from getting up so fast and I felt slightly nauseous.

"'Good morning, Mama' would be nice. Girl, ain't I teach you no manners!?" Mama Rose asked, pushing me to the side and walking in, uninvited.

"Good morning, Mama. It's just that I was still sleeping, so I'm a little out of sorts."

"Well, you better find your sorts 'cause I didn't raise none of my children to be so damn rude, especially to they own kin. Where's that husband of yours?"

Mama Rose made her way to the kitchen, opened the refrigerator and started pouring herself a glass of orange juice.

"Jayson's upstairs, asleep," I answered, wishing I was still in bed myself.

"So, the snake managed to slither his way home," Mama Rose retorted loudly.

"Mama Rose, can you please lower your voice?" I pleaded looking over my shoulder and up the stairs to our bedroom. I hoped Jayson had not awoken and heard Mama Rose referring to him as a 'slithering snake'.

"And just so you know, Jayson and I are doing just fine. He is taking me out to a nice restaurant for dinner this evening and he even agreed to let me go out with Myeisha afterwards. He thought it would be a good idea for me to have some girl time."

"What you mean, he agreed to *let* you go out tonight? Hell will freeze over and the devil will dance a jig the day a man *lets* me do a damn thing! I swear I raised you better than to be running up behind these no-good ass niggas!" Mama Rose boomed.

Her voice was getting louder by the second and I was scared Jayson would come down the stairs at any moment.

"So, is it just black men you don't like?" I asked, referring to her racial slur. "Would you have preferred if I had married another race...maybe a white man?"

"Dear lord, you are stupider than I thought," she sighed. "A man is a man no matter what color he is; they all the same. The only difference is black men kick they women out on the street when they done with them and the white men just kill theirs," Mama Rose professed as she slammed her empty juice glass down on the counter.

My headache was getting bigger by the second. I grabbed a bottle of Tylenol out of the cabinet and swallowed two pills with only a tenth of an ounce of water from my cupped hand. Just as I thought things couldn't get any worse, Jayson sauntered down the stairs wrapped in a dark blue terry robe.

"Good morning, my two sunshines,' Jayson greeted us. Even though he had just crawled out of bed, he looked wide awake and gorgeous, as usual. "What calls for this lucky visit?" he asked, kissing Mama Rose on the cheek.

"Hello, Jayson. I was just telling this wife of yours how she needs to have a decent breakfast cooking for her man when he gets up. A good man like you deserves to wake up to the smell of fresh biscuits and the sound of sizzling bacon," Mama Rose said, smiling from ear to ear.

Mama Rose's drastic change in demeanor was not shocking. I had seen her do it so many times as a child and as an adult. She could easily adjust her personality to her surroundings, almost like a chameleon. In the past, I had seen her go from laughing to crying hysterically or from stern to sweet as apple pie in the blink of an eye. She could play the role like an A-list actress. If I had finished my degree in Psychology, I'm sure she would have made a good study subject for bipolar disorders. It was obvious that Jayson had no clue that she had referred to him as a cold-blooded reptile less than two minutes ago; his cheesy grin assured me of that. This woman deserved an Oscar award.

"I think maybe I should be fixing her breakfast in bed to make up for all the time I've been spending at work," Jayson said, walking over to me and wrapping his arms around my shoulder.

"Well, that's part of being the wife of a respected attorney. We all have to make sacrifices," Mama Rose sang.

If she weren't my own mother, I might not have been able to fight the intense urge I had to slap her across the face. For a moment, I even envisioned using the pearl necklace hanging from her neck to choke her.

"And I appreciate her patience in putting up with me these days," Jayson said. "I'm working on a really difficult case and things have been pretty crazy around here, but as soon as this case is over, I'm taking my baby on a vacation. Anywhere in the whole entire world she wants to go."

"You are truly a good man, Jayson. My daughter is lucky to have you," Mama Rose said, with a fake smile plastered on her face.

I could not take one more minute of her shit.

"Mama Rose, I know you didn't come here because I make the best orange juice in the world," I stated, sarcastically.

"You're right about that," she snapped. "As a matter of fact, *we* have some important business to take care of this morning. You must have forgotten, dear. I'll remind you about it in the car, but we have to get going right now."

I didn't know what Mama Rose had up her sleeve, but I was sure nothing good was to come of it.

"Mama Rose, we don't have anything to do this morning. I surely would have remembered if we had something important scheduled," I argued.

"Well, you did forget and we have to get going now!" Mama Rose exclaimed forcefully.

"I have to get ready to head in for work anyways, so you two ladies go handle your business and be safe," Jayson said, kissing me on the lips and heading back upstairs.

As soon as Jayson left, I gave Mama Rose a spiteful glare.

"That's no way to look at your Mama," she sneered. "Now run upstairs and get changed into something nice. We have business to handle."

Chapter 7

"You have visitors," the nurse announced to the shadow hiding behind the curtain. I could make-out the outline of an old man's head through the thin white sheet that separated him from us. I could tell he was lying, half propped up, in a hospital bed.

My heart was beating so quickly that I thought I might have to tell the nurse to stand-by, in case I needed some assistance. Mama Rose had chosen today to tell me that my father, who I believed to be dead since I was eight years old, was actually still alive. He was dying, but still alive. Of course, Mama Rose had callously announced it in the car ride over, as if she were announcing that McDonald's was having a two for one sale on cheeseburgers. Since it was the second time that I had wanted to hit her in the short span of one hour, the urge was getting harder to resist.

There wasn't much I remembered about my father since my mother had made a point of not talking about him that much. My memories of him had long ago faded, but I always carried an old black and white photograph of him in my wallet. In the picture, he looked happy and strong standing next to my sister. They almost looked like twins in the photo, but I'm sure, twenty years later, a lot had changed.

According to Mama Rose, he had run off with some other lady and she had made up the story about him dying so we would not have to live with the shame that our own father did not want us. She stated that when he recently found out that he was dying of lung disease and his wife left him, he contacted my mother for help. She also added that he had owned a very lucrative business back in the day and had made a fortune that he wanted to leave to me and my sister.

All of the news was so overwhelming. What would I say to my father who I thought had been dead for years? What was even more incredible was that I would have to suffer through his death twice.

"Go on and say hello to your father, Genevieve," Mama Rose said, pushing me towards the curtain.

"Give me a second, Mama Rose," I urged. "This is very emotional for me."

"Come on now," Mama Rose said taking me by the hand and pulling me toward the curtain. "He ain't got long to live. Matter of fact, the doctors says he probably won't make it past this weekend." She yanked the curtain back, revealing the shell of a man. All that remained of my father was a thin layer of worn skin draped over a skeleton. I gasped and turned to run. I didn't know where I was going to go, but I felt like all of a sudden, there was not enough air in the room for me, my mother, and my father. Mama Rose grabbed me by the arm to stop my dash from the room.

"It's bad enough that he won't get to see Georgette since she done up and moved to the other side of the U.S. I know it's hard for you, but you need to at least give your daddy the courtesy of saying good-bye to him," Mama Rose said, pulling a chair up to the bed.

"You're right," I said. I stood over the bed, working up the nerve to actually focus my eyes on him and say "hello".

"Gen...ev...ieve," my father whispered. My name fell from his lips like a leaf from a tree. If I wasn't standing so close to him, I would have thought that he had only let out a small sigh.

"Your mother has told me so much about you," he said, taking a breath in between nearly every word. "I feel bad for missing out on your entire life. I want you to have everything when I pass. I made sure that you will."

"You don't have to apologize, Father. Please save your breaths," I begged. I could tell each breath took great effort. I held his bony hands and stared at him, trying to recall my memories of him as a child. He didn't look anything like he had in the picture; the disease had obviously transformed him into a mere smudge of the man he had once been.

"I'm glad you got to finally see your father," Mama Rose announced, standing up. "I think we should leave now and let him get some rest."

I squeezed his hand one last time before following her out of the room.

We didn't speak to each other on the elevator or as we walked through the hospital lobby. I had to bite my tongue to stop from calling her a few choice words. I was glad she had driven because I was too much of a wreck to concentrate on driving. We were only a couple of blocks from the hospital before I finally burst out in tears.

"Genevieve, clam down. It's really not that serious," Mama Rose stated.

"How can you say that? I finally meet the father that I thought was dead, only to find out that he is dying."

"Girl, that ain't none of your daddy."

"Wh... What do you mean?" I stuttered, utterly confused.

"Your daddy, the sorry bastard, was Elroy Johnson. He died when you were eight years old. Georgette will confirm that. That man back there in the hospital room was Jim McPherson. I made him think you and Georgette was his long lost children so he would leave all his money to y'all."

"You have got be kidding me!" I screamed. "Either that or you're just pure evil."

"Evil!?" she yelled. "That man was going to die all alone with no family. He was an old man with no offspring and no one to love him. We had an affair for many years when I was married to your daddy. Your daddy was too busy running around, sleeping with every whore in Memphis, to pay me any attention, so I got it from him. Jim could have been your daddy, 'cept for he as sterile as a horse with one nut and he knows it. He believed my lie 'cause he wanted to. So, I say, who am I to take a dying man's dream to have a family from him?"

I could only stare at her.

"It's a win-win situation," Mama Rose stated calmly.

"I can't believe you," I cried.

"And I can't believe you was fool enough to believe that was your Daddy," Mama Rose laughed.

Chapter 8

I decided not to tell Jayson about my mother's crazy stunt this morning. I was too excited about our dinner date and didn't want to ruin the evening with my mother's nonsense. Since Jayson was an attorney, I was sure he could inform me of the legal ramifications of my mother's crazy scheme, but as much as she drove me bonkers, I didn't want to see her in jail.

Jayson pulled up to the front of Romano's. I could smell the food from the valet station. With my mother nowhere in sight, I planned on eating any and everything but a salad.

"I'm glad we were finally able to steal some time and sneak away," he said, opening my car door.

I was more than glad, I was grateful for the chance to salvage our relationship. Jayson was on his best behavior. He was paying close attention to me, making sure I felt like I was the only thing that mattered to him that night. He even went as far as to leave his Blackberry on the kitchen counter at home, so there would be no interruptions. Even when Bret had called, right before we left the house to advise Jayson about an unexpected turn in a case, Jayson brushed him off and told him that he would discuss the matter with him in the morning.

Saturday night at Romano's was hectic and every seat was taken. The servers were maneuvering through the tables and crowd with precision. Jayson's foresight to make reservations meant that we were promptly whisked past the line of anxious patrons to a private candlelight table in the back, away from the sounds of clanging dishes and boisterous chatter.

"Perfect," Jayson said to the host while handing him a folded bill. Jayson tipped well, so we could always count on good service. The waiter was at our table with hot bread, olive oil and seasoning before we could settle into our seats. Within minutes, our wine had arrived and the waiter had rushed off to place our orders.

"It really has been a long time since we've spent some quality time together," Jayson said, adjusting in his seat. "I'm really sorry about how things have been going lately. Everything has been so hectic at the office that I've been ignoring what truly matters - home." He was making the sorry puppy-dog face, the one that made me forgive any and everything.

"I think I could be a little more understanding about your obligations. After all, I knew what I was getting into when I married an attorney," I said, trying to be an understanding wife. Our unofficial agreement to both try to make things work seemed to be all we needed to move on. We were so busy laughing and carrying on that the wine bottles seemed to empty themselves. The food was amazing, as usual, but since I was already full of wine, I was barely able to finish my entrée and dessert was out of the question.

I noticed Jayson tried to steer clear of the subject of work. I didn't want him to feel so uncomfortable that he could not confide in me about his career, something that was so much a part of him.

"So, what's this new case that's been taking up all your time about?" I asked, finishing off my umpteenth glass of Moscato.

"You sure you want to discuss work," Jayson said, arching his left eyebrow like he always did when he was confused or unsure.

"Yes, I'm really interested in whatever it is that seems to be occupying you lately. I mean, you've had some really difficult cases before, but none that have required this much of your time," I said softly, trying not to sound accusing or too prying.

"Well, I'm actually glad you asked. I've been dying to run the details by someone who's not a part of the firm - someone unbiased."

"Shoot, I'm all ears."

"Well, our client is a thirty-year-old husband and father of two. He works for the city garbage disposal on the night shift, driving the garbage truck. When another driver calls in sick, he offers to cover the shift on his day off. He's doing his pick-ups when a car pulls up next to him. Our client is distracted, adjusting the radio, so he doesn't notice that a man has jumped out of the car next to him and is now at the window, holding a gun to his head. The masked man demands that our client hand over the "shit". Apparently, there's something in the truck that this guy wants, so my client fishes around under the seat, in the glove compartment, behind the sun visor - anywhere that he thinks someone might hide something. He's searching like crazy for whatever it is that this guy wants. The guy is yelling at him, telling him if he doesn't hurry up and give him "the shit," he's going to blow his brains out. He even starts counting down backwards from ten. Our client finally finds something under the seat, but I don't think it was what this guy was looking for or wanted. Our client finds a .357 magnum under the seat and shoots the masked man in his face before the man can shoot him. Now, he's being charged with first degree murder."

"It sounds more like self-defense," I said, stating the obvious.

"The problem is that the gun belonged to our client, even though he claims he doesn't know how it got there. So, the case is being treated more like a botched drug deal. When we asked our client if he's noticed anything strange leading up to the event, he stated that for a few months prior to this incident, he suspected his wife was having an affair with someone at his job. On several occasions, he noticed his work number on her cell phone during dates and times that he knew he had not called her from work. When he confronted her about the calls, she tried to convince him that he had called her from work those times, but he knew it wasn't the truth."

"Do you think she set him up?" I gasped.

"I guess we're on the same page because that's exactly what I think," Jayson stated. "My theory is Mrs. Westings was creeping around with one of her husband's co-workers for probably more than just a few months. However long it was it was, it was enough time for them to fall in love and decide to try to have Mr. Westings permanently removed from the picture. The fact that my client was covering for another co-worker that night and driving a garbage route that he normally would not have taken indicates that someone was setting him up. Most likely, the very same co-worker that my client was generously covering the shift for is the same person who is sleeping with his wife and the same one that was trying to set him up."

I really felt bad for Mr. Westings. "I am glad he has someone as dedicated as you fighting for him. It sounds like your theory is pretty plausible."

"A theory is just that Genevieve - a theory. It's possible, but I have to prove every single bit of it to the judge to get my client's case dismissed. The driver in the car with the gunman took off and my client was unable to get the license plate. With no witnesses and a dead gunman that we can't yet tie to anyone at his workplace, there's not much to go off of."

"Does Bret agree with you on the theory?" I asked.

Jayson laughed. "Bret is usually one of the main persons I rely on in the firm to help me in difficult cases like this. He's never been a good lead attorney. Paperwork and legalities isn't really his thing. But, he's an awesome fact-finder and prefers to do the leg work in cases. He likes to collect the evidence and investigate, but his head has been in the clouds lately. He told me he met someone special. Whoever she is, she must be one bad-ass female because for the last few days, his head seems like it screwed on backwards."

It was obvious that Bret's recent behavior was causing delays in the case. I couldn't help but feel happy for Bret. I couldn't recall the last time he had been in a relationship. As a matter of fact, the last time I had ever seen him with someone was at me and Jayson's wedding. I thought the tall, slender brunette that had accompanied him was beautiful and they seemed compatible, but she soon became nothing more than a memory and a photo in my wedding album.

"I understand it's interfering with work, but you have to consider that Bret has given up a lot of his social life for his career. I am happy he finally met someone. You're his best friend, Jayson. You should be happy for him, too," I chastised.

"You're right. I am happy for him. And get this: she's a sista. I always knew Bret preferred his coffee black,"

"I'll have to tell Myeisha she lost out and Bret is already taken," I giggled, taking a sip of wine.

"Don't jump the gun. I don't know how long things will last. He said she's married and she must have some nerve because he's been to her house already. He went on and on the other day about how she looked like a Victoria's secret model when she came to the door in her lingerie one night. A scandalous woman like that. I sure hope he know what he's getting in to," Jayson stated, wearily.

My mouthful of white wine spewed across the table. Some droplets leapt in the air landing on Jayson's blazer.

"Are you okay?" he asked, hopping up from his seat to aid me.

"Thanks, I um...I just had some wine go down the wrong pipe."

Jayson gently wiped the corner of my mouth with his napkin, then started dabbing at the spot on his jacket.

Jayson's comment had taken me off guard. I was hoping that it was just a coincidence that Bret had recently met a married, black woman that he was falling in love with who came to the door in her lingerie, but the more I thought about my run-in with Bret a few nights ago and the way his eyes had roamed my body and penetrated my soul, the more I knew it was far from a coincidence. I could even remember his breath on my neck, wispy and warm. For the rest of the night, I could barely look Jayson in the eye. God forbid he knew that I was that scandalous woman.

Chapter 9

I opened my mail box and everything from our phone bill to advertisements promising a free cruise if I signed up for a weight loss club fell onto the sidewalk. I scooped up the mass of once living trees and shuffled through each article.

"Trash... junk mail... more junk mail... bills," I murmured.

A manila envelope caught my eye. McPherson Trust was in place of the sender's name. The name rang a bell, but I couldn't recall where I had heard it from. Jayson usually didn't have packages from work delivered to the house, but it definitely looked like some sort of legal documents. I put it on the top of the pile and headed into the house.

Overall, things had gone very well last night at dinner. Jayson and I were able to spend some much needed one-on-one time together and he was able to discuss the case that was weighing so heavily on his mind with me. The fact that he had listened intently to my opinion regarding the case was flattering. I wanted him to feel that he could come to me, his wife, for anything. I had met some of the other attorney's wives at a Christmas party the firm hosted last year in the Hilton ballroom. Most of them were Las Vegas trophy wives – beautiful, but with no ambition of their own, other than shopping for clothes and their next nip and tuck. I was sure their husbands didn't feel comfortable enough to discuss intricate murder cases with them. I was proud that mine did.

The phone rang and I cringed. I knew I had to face Myeisha's wrath for skipping out on our plans to go out after dinner, but the party me and Jayson had in the bedroom last night was more fun than Myeisha could match at any strip club. I picked up the phone and took in a deep breath bracing myself for Myeisha's grilling.

"Hello, honey, how are you today?" the voice from the other end sang. It took me a second to work through the confusion before I could respond. The voice was very familiar; one that I had known since childhood. It was no doubt Mama Rose's, but I had never heard her sound so pleasant or refer to me as honey before. Without the usual angst in her voice, it was difficult to accept this as being my mother on the other end.

"Mama Rose?"

"Yes, it's me, sweetie," she replied.

"Sorry, you just sound so..." I struggled for a word to use that wouldn't offend her. "You sound like you're in a really good mood."

"Well, is there a reason that I should be in a bad mood today?"

"No, not at all," I responded, still thrown off by her abnormal cheerful behavior.

"Well, I just called to see how my daughter was doing today. I know Jayson spends so much time away from home at the office, so I just wanted to check up on you."

I walked over to the bar and poured myself a small glass of scotch, even though it was well before noon. There was no question that before the phone call ended, I would find out the real reason for her call and it would not be all sunshine and roses.

"I'm doing fine. Was there something you needed?" I asked, refusing to continue to play this obnoxious game with her any longer. After the stunt she had pulled at the hospital, I had decided that I was not about to let her drag me into anymore of her malicious and dangerous games. I respected Mama Rose. She had raised me and my sister mostly on her own. There were aunts and uncles that popped in to make sure we were okay, but it was Mama Rose who worked double shifts at the hospital as a nurse to make sure that we had food in our bellies and a roof over our heads. When my father passed away, she had to add tending to our two acres of land to her already full "to do" list. No matter how many hours she worked at the hospital or how much dirt she had plowed that week, come Sunday, she made sure me and Georgette showed up to church in our finest clothes and with our hair all done up and fancy. She'd strut into the stuffy, overcrowded and dilapidated white building on the corner of Newman Street and 5th and brag to everyone from the choir boys to the preacher about her two adorable daughters. At home, we couldn't do nothing right, but at church, we were her two beautiful perfect angels. When my sister was in her late teens, she decided to openly display her affection towards the same sex. After Mama Rose recovered from the shock of her eldest daughter's choice in partners, we never saw the inside of that church on Newman and 5th again. Mama Rose packed everything up and we moved all the way across the country to Las Vegas, Nevada of all places, which always puzzled me. If she was trying to escape the wicked lure of sex, she had sure picked the wrong damn place to go. Of course, moving to Las Vegas did not change my sister's sexual preference and shortly thereafter, Georgette announced that, against my mother's will, she had chosen to attend Florida A&M College. Besides moving overseas, my sister couldn't have chosen anywhere further from my mother than Florida. I knew she did it on purpose and I couldn't blame her. There were many times that I regretted not making the same decision my sister had.

"Genevieve, why are you always so scrutinizing?" Mama Rose whined. "If you don't want me to call you then just say so. I have my friends from church who don't mind my company. Sister Marybelle may be hard of hearing, but she can read lips just fine and she thinks I'm better than butter on white bread. Sister Charlotte, too. Shoot, they're God-fearing Christian women who know good people when they see them and they like me just fine. Maybe I'll just go visit one of them since my own daughter ain't got no time for me."

"That's not what I meant, Mama. I'm sorry if that's how I sounded," I said, feeling guilty.

"Well, I'll let you get back to what you was so busy doing," Mama Rose said, despondently.

"Really, I wasn't *that* busy," I said, taking another sip of scotch.

"Oh, okay!" In that case, I was just wondering if you received anything... umm... interesting in the mail lately?" she asked.

"Interesting? Like, what?" I asked confused, but only for a moment before I looked over to the stack of mail on the kitchen table. The manila envelope sat on top. Jim McPherson. That was the name of the man my mother had taken me to see in the hospital. The man who, the last time I saw him, lay withering away to nothing on a dingy bed sheet. It was also the name on the package I had just received in the mailbox.

"Interesting like something you wouldn't normally receive any other day like a special delivery!" she yelled, sounding irritated. She was beginning to sound more and more like the Mama Rose I knew.

"Not today and I'd better get back to what I was busy doing," I said hurriedly before saying goodbye and hanging up, leaving her no time to respond.

I grabbed the large rectangular envelope and used a letter opener to make one long slit from one end of it to the other. There was a check inside. I had to recount the number of zeros that followed the number two on the check. The fourth time I did so confirmed that I had just received a check in my name from Jim McPherson in the amount of 2 million dollars.

Even though I knew Jim McPherson wasn't my father, I shivered at the fact that me holding this check in my hand at this moment meant that he was now dead. He had probably died right after me and my mother's visit. I despised my mother for dragging me into her mess. With my previous stint in jail, I did not want to take any chances getting caught up in something illegal and immoral, to say the least.

I did not want this on my conscience, but two million dollars was a lot of money and according to my mother, he had no other family to pass his fortune on to. If he hadn't left it to me, he probably would have just donated it to some charity like Easter Seal or The Red Cross, who wouldn't have done anything but padded their pockets with the fortune. After reasoning with my conscience, I folded the check and hid it safely underneath my panties in my oak dresser, making sure to shred the envelope it came in. Until I made a decision on what to do with the check, its spot beneath my silk thongs and lace bras was as safe a hiding place as any.

Chapter 10

Myeisha dropped by my house after she got off work later that afternoon. I was glad to see that she was too excited about her newest strip club adventure to be mad at me.

"Girl, I knew you was going to chicken out at the last minute anyways," she said, opening my refrigerator and making herself a salami and cheese sandwich.

"I went with Candace instead. We got home so late that I barely made it to work this morning. My dumb ass boss was riding me all morning long about some new procedure they implemented at the bank in case of a robbery. If we do get held up, I'm gonna tell the robber that the key to the big safe is in that bitch's bra," she said smacking loudly. "I don't know how her senile ass got promoted over me anyways."

Even though Myeisha always said her boss, who was an older, cranky, bitter widower, always picked on her, it was her boss that I really felt sorry for. Myeisha was strong and sharp enough to stick up for herself. However, when Myeisha had a disliking for someone, she had a tendency to make that person's life miserable. If it wasn't for the fact that she was the top teller and the only employee knowledgeable enough to manage the bank in her boss's absence, I'm sure she would have been fired a long time ago. When she and Jayson first met, it was a full-time job to stop her from telling him how much she couldn't stand him. "He's an arrogant jack-ass who thinks money and prestige is a substitute for common courtesy and manners," she had told me on many occasions.

She was only able to stay civil with him out of respect for our friendship. To this day, when he's not looking, she sometimes flips him the bird behind his back.

"So, was Chocolate Milk stripping last night?" I asked.

"It's Hot Chocolate and no, he wasn't there last night, but Caramel Craze was filling in for him and he did a damn good job. He was so good that I had to purchase a private dance and it was well worth it."

"With names like Hot Chocolate and Caramel Craze, you might as well buy a candy bar to get your fix."

"Hershey's ain't got nothing on them," Myeisha moaned. "But enough about me. How did dinner go last night with the hubby?"

"It went really good, considering I think his best friend has a crush on me," I said.

"You've got to be freaking kidding me!" Myeisha screamed. She quickly covered her mouth and looked over her shoulder towards the foyer as if she were expecting someone to walk in.

"Don't worry Jayson isn't here, he's at work," I said, understanding the reason for her nervousness.

"Does Jayson know?" Myeisha spoke in a hushed tone, even though I had just told her we were the only people in the house.

"He's the one who told me. He told me that Bret seems preoccupied with some married African-American woman, but he doesn't know that woman is me yet."

"How do you know that woman is you, if that's all that Jayson said?"

"Because of what happened last week when Bret came over and saw me…" I cleared me throat and shifted my eye contact away from Myeisha and onto a brass hour glass on top of the fireplace mantle. "Well, he kinda saw me half naked."

"You little slut! I always knew you had it in you," Myeisha said, bent over in laughter.

"It's not even like that! He came over to give me a message from Jayson. I wasn't expecting him at the door; I was expecting Jayson and Bret just happened to catch a little sneak peak."

"Sure, whatever," Myeisha said still laughing. Apparently the situation was more than amusing to her. "So, now that you have got this white boy whipped, what are you going to do about it?"

"What do you mean, what am I going to do? I'm going to talk to him like a grown adult and explain to him that this whole thing is absolutely ridiculous. He's Jayson's best friend and it would really hurt Jayson if he knew his best man at his wedding wanted to be with his wife. I have no interest in Bret and maybe if I tell him that to his face, he won't bring the subject up to Jayson anymore."

"So, when do you plan on doing this?" Myeisha asked, making herself welcome to my last bottle of pomegranate juice in the refrigerator. I snatched the bottle from her hand, mid-pour.

"Whoa, excuse me, you adulteress, you," Myeisha snickered.

"Actually, I don't have anything on my agenda tomorrow. I think I'll phone Bret today and schedule a friendly lunch with him tomorrow afternoon. We are both mature adults, I'm sure we can resolve this little issue in no time," I stated confidently. "Or maybe my assumption is totally wrong and it's not me at all." I was honestly hoping for the latter.

"Are we still going forward with our plan on Friday?" Myeisha asked. "Candace needs to know if she supposed to go to Posh."

With everything going on, I had already forgot about our plan to set Jayson up. Dinner had gone pretty good the other night, but that wasn't enough to convince me that nothing else was going on. I could not deny my urge to see just how Jayson would react if he was seduced by a sexy young vixen like Candace. Hopefully, he would brush her off and we could go on with our happy lives.

"Sure, tell her Posh, Friday, 6:00 pm sharp."

Myeisha picked up her phone to confirm the date with Candace. While she was busy, I made a phone call of my own.

"Hello, Franklin and Franklin Law Firm. How may I direct your call?" the monotone voice on the other end asked.

"Can you please connect me to the secretary for Attorney Bret Stephenson?"

"Sure, hold for just one moment, please."

"Hello, you've reached Attorney Bret Stephenson's office. How can I be of assistance?"

"Hi, I'm a very important previous client of Mr. Stephenson's and I wanted to surprise him with lunch tomorrow at Spago's at around 2:00 pm," I said quickly, thinking of a nice restaurant that didn't require reservations.

"Let me check his agenda, ma'am," she said, placing me on hold. "His schedule is clear for that time, but who shall I tell him his reservation is with?"

"I'm Ms. Johnson," I said, thinking of a common last name. "He may not remember me, but I'm sure he will when he sees me."

"Okay, Ms. Johnson. I have Mr. Stephenson down for lunch tomorrow at Spago's at 2:00pm."

"Sounds perfect."

Chapter 11

I sat on the edge of my bed with my hand on the phone receiver. I couldn't think of anyone else other than my sister to talk to about my mother's latest scandal. It had been a couple of months since we had last spoken. At that time, her longtime girlfriend, Adrianna, had just moved in with her. They had even been discussing marriage.

"Gen!" she exclaimed as soon as she heard my voice.

"Hey, Georgette, how are things with you and Adrianna?"

"She's still trying to convince me to get married and I'm still trying to convince her to slow her roll. What's up with you lil' sis? Is Mr. Big Stuff Attorney treating you right?"

"Everything in that department seems to be going okay, but what I really called you about is Mom."

"Go figure. Mama Rose is at it again, huh?"

"Yeah, but this time she's really gotten herself in deep and she's dragging me in with her. Earlier today, I received a check for 2 million dollars from some poor old guy that Mama Rose had convinced I was his daughter. She even tricked me into going to the hospital to see him on his death bed."

"Well, well, well, she hasn't slowed down, even in her old age."

"You don't sound surprised at all."

"Gen, Mama Rose has been dragging me in her shit for as long as I can remember. You were too young, so Mama Rose always used me in her little twisted schemes, but I guess you have been officially recruited now."

"You say it like Mama Rose has been conning people her whole life."

"She's been doing more than conning folks. That lady is pure evil, plain and simple. If you know what's best for you, you would get far away from her. That man of yours makes descent money. Why don't ya'll pack up and move to Virginia or something. I heard they have lovely beaches."

I had come to Georgette for a simple solution to end Mama Rose's plots and schemes and here she was, telling me to pack my belonging and relocate to the East Coast as the answer.

"Well, what do you think I should do about the check?" I asked, still searching for some guidance.

"I think you should burn it and erase it from your memory. It was wrong for her to bring you in on her nonsense. And Gen, I love you, but please do not call me about Mama Rose again. I do not want to be implicated in any of her scam jobs. Unless that lady is breathing her last breath, don't call me about her again." Georgette's harsh words were followed by complete silence and then, a dial tone.

I understood what Georgette was saying about my mother's questionable character, however, I did think she was overreacting. Why would she say she didn't want to see Mama Rose unless she was dying? Georgette's behavior was disrespectful and disturbing. I wouldn't dare hurt Mama Rose's feelings and tell her what Georgette had just said. I knew Mama Rose was a bit irrational and over-the-top, but I didn't think she deserved to be referred to with such contempt from her own daughter. I guess going to Georgette had not been the right decision after all.

I heard Jayson's footsteps coming up the stairs to the bedroom. I was ecstatic that he had actually made it home before I fell asleep.

"Hey, baby. How was your day?" Jayson asked, throwing his weathered brown suitcase on top of the ottoman at the end of the bed.

I tried to erase the conversation I had just had with Georgette out of my head and act normal.

"Myeisha came over to visit earlier, but other than that, it was a pretty uneventful day," I said, getting out of bed and throwing my arms over his wide shoulders. His navy blue suit jacket held the familiar scent of his aftershave - a hypnotizing light musk. There were no traces of the floral fragrance that I had smelled on him a few weeks ago.

Jayson nestled his head into my hair. Everything felt right again, like when we first met. I felt optimistic that my recent fears that Jayson was cheating were incorrect. Now that he had opened up to me about the complexity and seriousness of his current case, I understood his aloofness and could rationalize the extra time he spent away from home. Within seconds, both of our clothes lay scattered across the floor. We fell onto the bed, grasping at each frantically. His tongue searched every inch of my body until I was floating in pure ecstasy. We explored each other as if we had discovered unchartered territory. I could not remember the last time our lovemaking had been so passionate and fulfilling. Afterward, we lay tangled in the sheets, completed exhausted. He quickly dozed off while I crawled out of the bed for a warm shower. When I returned, Jayson was sprawled across the bed, snoring loudly. Every inch of the bed was covered by one of his massive limbs. He moaned and a wide smile spread across his face in his sleep. I laughed to myself and lifted his arm, gently sliding in underneath it. Jayson instinctively turned to the side and pulled me into his body. I scooted back until the curve of my butt rested perfectly in his pelvis. Jayson moaned again. Even though I had just thoroughly enjoyed myself, I hoped he was not ready for round two because I was completely drained. He started snoring again and I began dozing off.

"Mmm..." Jason moaned again. I continued to fade away as exhaustion swallowed me.

"Mmm... Lisa."

The haziness was so thick that I wasn't quite sure if the barely audible whisper had come from Jayson or from a thought somewhere deep within my dreams. I lay there, suspended in a fog somewhere between sleep and consciousness before the darkness prevailed and I slipped away.

Chapter 12

There had to be more to life than sitting around trying to detect traces of Jayson's infidelity. I lay in bed, pretending to be asleep while Jayson got dressed for work the next morning. The whole time I lay there, I tried to replay whatever it was I had heard him moan in his sleep. I was so consumed in it that an hour later when I heard Jayson pull out of the driveway, I was still stuck on the same thought. To snap out of my rut, I decided to stop by the hair salon for a wash and deep condition. Not only was my hair in critical need of some TLC by my beautician, Neeka, but I also needed her ear and sound advice. As soon as I walked in the busy salon, I knew there would be a long wait. I had not made an appointment because, as a faithful client, Neeka always found a way to fit me in.

"Hey, girl, how is that fine ass husband of yours doing?" Jordan, another beautician in the shop, asked. I picked up a magazine and pretended to be so engrossed in its contents that I had not heard her question.

Jordan was a gossipy, malicious socialite who could spread a rumor faster than fire through a haystack. With her extra-wide hips, pox-marked skin and a mass of wild, untamed hair that she had the nerve to dye cherry-red, she was also an eye-sore. It amazed me that people saw the mess on top of her head and still trusted her to style their precious locks.

"She knows she heard me. I can't stand stuck-up people," Jordan loudly whispered to the client in her chair as she braided her hair. She couldn't stand stuck-up people and I couldn't stand loud-mouthed, ignorant, shit-starters like her.

I put the magazine down on the table, ready to tell her a thing or two, when the receptionist walked up and handed me a bottle of water.

"Hello, Ms. Mitchell. Neeka is just finishing her last client's appointment, then she'll be right with you. Would like to wait up front or would you like me to escort you to the back?" the young, exceptionally thin receptionist asked.

"I'll wait in the back," I said, throwing Jordan a nasty glare before following the receptionist to the back. If Myeisha was here she probably would have tried to slap Jordan across the face with one of the smoking hot straightening combs on the counter. After three years of coming to Jordan to get her hair done, Myeisha had been wronged by her. Jordan had broken the unwritten vow of secrecy that every hairdresser shares with their clients. Not only had she told all of Myeisha's business that Myeisha had shared with her in confidence over the years, but she had exaggerated on most of it and fabricated tidbits, making Myeisha look like she deserved the Skank of the Year Award.

"Go ahead and sit at the wash bowl. I'll be faster than you can blink," Neeka hollered across the room to me. Her heels clacked across the wooden floor as she rushed around taking the last few rollers out of her client's hair.

"Voila!" she exclaimed, spinning the chair around so her client could see the finished product. The young girl admired herself in the mirror before giving Neeka a tip and heading to the front to book her next appointment. Neeka was skillful with a comb and a pair of scissors. She was the best that Las Vegas had to offer. Unlike Jordan's tangled un-kept strands, Neeka's beautiful, jet black coils were always in perfect order. She was the reason why I had decided to quit the damaging perms and weaves and go natural. That was only two years ago and now, my kinks and curls were almost as luxurious and thick as hers.

"I think you're going to need one of my special conditioner cocktails today," Neeka announced, running her fingers through my dry curls.

"I didn't get a chance to come in last week for my usual. Things were kinda hectic at home."

"That's all right. I'll get you all fixed up in no time," Neeka said, massaging my scalp underneath the gentle flow of warm water. The tingle from the peppermint and tea tree oil shampoo was invigorating.

"So, what's going on at home that has you so preoccupied that you've been neglecting your mane?"

I was eager to get an outsider and neutral opinion of me and Jayson's situation. Myeisha's dislike of Jayson automatically put him in the doghouse with her. Mama Rose didn't trust any man other than God and Georgette was not someone I felt comfortable confiding in after our conversation last night.

"I don't know if I'm overreacting but…"

I looked around the room to make sure there weren't any nosey clients or hairdressers listening in on our conversation, Jordan, in particular. We were the only ones in the back shampoo room.

"Well, what would you think if your man came home smelling like petunias? That is, of course, when he actually brought his ass home. And get this shit... last night, after we made love, I could swear he moaned some bitch's name in his sleep."

"And that nigga still alive!?" Neeka exclaimed.

"Well, I was half asleep when I thought I heard him whisper something. It sounded like Melissa or Lisa, but I was so tired, he could've just been saying something else altogether. I could be throwing this whole thing way out of proportion."

"I would've cut him first and asked questions later, but that's just me."

I could totally get what she was saying. I would've done just that before, but I realized that inflicting physical pain would only be an immediate short-term solution. If Jayson really was sneaking around, I would make sure that he had so much more coming to him than just a few bumps and bruises. That would be so cliché: the scorned wife flailing madly at her cheating husband as she screams, "Why!?" There was no way he was getting away that easily. The price for betraying me would be much higher.

Two hours later, I looked and felt much better than I had in days. Neeka had worked her usual magic. My thick curls were back bouncy and shiny and our informal therapy session had lifted a heavy weight from my back.

"Thanks, Neeka," I said, giving her a hug before walking back up front to book my next appointment.

"My pleasure, honey, but make sure you come see me sooner than later next time," she said, folding up the forty dollar tip I had just handed her and stuffing it into her bra.

By the time I left the salon, there was only thirty minutes left until my lunch date with Bret at noon. It would be difficult for me to make it across town during lunchtime in such a short amount of time. Luckily, I had taken the Jaguar instead of our SUV. If I punched it, I could still make it to Spago's on time. I jumped into the driver's seat and adjusted my rearview mirror, admiring Neeka's work before sliding on my seatbelt. The intense sensation of eyes burning a hole into me caused me to take one last look at the salon before pulling off. Jordan was standing right outside the salon door, smoking a cigarette. The red pumps that she had managed to stuff her plump feet into matched her flaming red hair. Our eyes locked. She flicked her cigarette on the ground with her long, bright yellow nail, then smashed it into the ground with her heels. She smiled at me, but there was nothing friendly about the sinister smirk on her lips. I didn't like Jordan for what she had done to my friend, however, I was unsure of why Jordan didn't like me. Maybe it was because I had everything she probably wanted but couldn't have: a nice figure, a fine husband, a bad ass car and hair that didn't look like a damn bird's nest. There was one thing I was sure of: the next time I came for my appointment, if she even looked at me cross-eyed, some shit was going to go down. Oh So Natural was the salon I had been going to for the last three years now, way before Jordan's fat ass had even started working there. If she thought she was intimidating me, she had another thing coming. I returned her smirk by flipping her off as I backed out of my parking space. Her mouth hung open in disbelief of my gesture. I turned up my radio and blocked out the obscenities she screamed as I drove away, bopping my head to the music. I had bigger fish to fry and a lunch date with my husband's best friend.

Chapter 13

I was a woman on a mission. Bret would have no choice but to abandon his fixation with me. If Jayson ever figured out that the married woman Bret liked was me and the reason why Bret liked me was because he had seen me nearly naked, then I would have a lot of explaining to do. It would be my word against Bret's if Bret continued to feed Jayson stories about this "married woman," then told him it was actually me. Regardless of the fact that I was telling the truth, Jayson would have a hard time believing me since I made the mistake of not telling him the truth from the beginning.

My plan was to wear something seductive enough to get him to stay and talk, then let him down slowly. I had chosen to wear a fitted white wrap dress and my gold 6-inch Manolo heels to meet Bret in. My new hairstyle added the perfect touch to my outfit. All the men's heads turned as the host escorted me to the table where Bret was waiting. One lady even threw her napkin at her husband when his gaze followed me past their table.

Bret looked pleasantly surprised, but jumbled when I arrived at the table. He jumped up from his seat to pull my chair out for me, nearly tripping over his own two feet as he did so.

"Thank you," I said, as he pushed my chair up to the table.

"I thought I was meeting an old client of mine. I wasn't expecting you. Is Jayson joining us too?" Bret looked hesitant and confused.

"I'm really sorry for making up a lie to get you here, but I wanted to be inconspicuous. And no, Jayson won't be joining us," I replied, shaking my head. I expected him to be angry that I had lied in order to get him here. Instead, all signs of anxiety left his face and were replaced with sheer excitement and joy. He relaxed and lent back in his chair.

"You look absolutely stunning."

"Thanks," I said purposefully withholding any comment about his appearance. Bret looked undeniably handsome himself. I was starting to see what Myeisha was talking about. His tailored Armani suit fit his tall, slender body perfectly. The ocean blue tie he was wearing made his eyes sparkle. He reminded me of Brad Pitt. It wasn't just the sandy, blonde hair and his sky blue eyes, but Bret was the perfect package of gorgeous, suave and edgy, all rolled up into one.

The waiter came and we placed our orders. Mama Rose would have been proud because although Spago's was my second favorite restaurant, after Romano's, I only ordered a salad and tea.

"I hope you are not on a diet. Your figure is already perfect," he said, smiling and staring me directly in the eye. There was something about the way that he looked at me that left me feeling totally exposed. The feeling was not degrading, but intensely sensual. I blushed and began to second guess my choice in clothing today.

"I'm always watching my weight and making sure I am in shape, but diets really aren't my thing," I said, taking a sip of water.

"Well, that's good to hear. I hate those women that think starving themselves is appealing. I much prefer the softness, curves and shape of a woman with a little meat on her bones," he said while erotically tracing the length of his wine glass with his fingertip. Why hadn't I noticed before how everything about this man was mischievous and alluring? All of a sudden, my palms were sweaty and my cheeks were burning. I could clearly see in which direction Bret was heading.

Our meeting was spiraling out of control and our food had not even arrived at the table yet. I had to regain power over the situation quickly before he tried to take things to another level.

"Look, Bret, I wanted to see you today because I think that after that night when I came to the door… uhm… not fully dressed, I think you may have gotten the wrong idea."

"I don't think I got the wrong idea. Remember, I am an attorney and therefore, I am pretty good at the art of reasoning and deduction. I know you were expecting Jayson and not me."

"Well, why are you telling Jayson that you are having an affair with some married lady?"

"I didn't tell Jayson I was having an affair with some married lady. I told him that I was in love with a married woman."

"Does that have anything to do with that night?"

I was beginning to feel embarrassed. Maybe I *had* gotten the wrong impression and Bret was actually talking about some other lady. I was hoping that he would tell me I was a complete nut for making such an assumption. We could have a good laugh, then I would beg him not to tell Jayson about the other night or today and we could both move on with our lives.

"It had nothing to do with the other night," he laughed.

I breathed a sigh of relief and quietly cursed myself for jumping to conclusions.

"It has everything to do with how I have felt about you since the first time I laid eyes on you," Bret continued.

I gasped and sat frozen in shock.

"Jayson doesn't deserve you. He's a fool that takes advantage of everything he has simply because he thinks it's owed to him. You deserve someone who will be there for you, someone who will be eagerly waiting at the table when you cook dinner, someone to protect you and lay in bed with you every night. Jayson's only true love is his career. He will never be able to love you the way I can," Bret stated boldly.

"I love Jayson," I declared, responding with the only thought that came to my head.

"I don't question your love for him. It is his love for you that I am unsure of. Haven't you doubted it yourself?"

It was as if he was reading my every fear for the last few months. Of course I had questioned Jayson's love for me. From the time he came home smelling like perfume to the time he moaned some bitch's name in his sleep, I wondered if I was just a person of convenience to him. I had tried to convince myself that I was just being paranoid but I was really in denial. If Jayson's best-friend, Myeisha and Mama Rose could see it, then I guess I was the only blind one in the pack, but I refused to be blind any longer.

"I didn't come here to discuss me and Jayson's relationship."

"Then, what exactly did you come here for?" Bret asked, leaning across the table and touching my hand.

I didn't utter a word, but we both understood what was transpiring. The fact that I allowed his hand to linger on top of mine without pulling back, the knowing in both of our eyes as we stayed locked in each other's gaze said enough. We had both just made a silent agreement to betray someone very close to both of us.

Chapter 14

I could tell it had been a long time since Bret had been with a woman. His eagerness showed from the moment he tossed two hundred dollar bills on the table before receiving our food fleeing Spago's to now as he impatiently peeled off every piece of my clothing in the hotel room.

Jayson had been my only lover for years, but allowing myself to succumb to Bret was easier than I had imagined. He was much more forceful in bed than Jayson… and I liked it. I didn't have to wonder what Bret liked because he showed me by manipulating my body into whichever position he wanted to try next. After trying several positions, he bent me over the side of the bed and entered me from behind, pulling my hair gently as he did so. We came together as he pulled me to his chest and grunted my name. A part of me felt guilty until I recalled how Jayson had just moaned someone else's name in his sleep just last night. He had it coming, but I bet he wasn't expecting me to be better at his own game than he was.

Bret called his secretary and told her that he had eaten something that had upset his stomach at lunch, so he would not be in for the rest of the day. We ended up having sex in the shower, on the hotel balcony and dining room table. Hours had passed before I realized that light had faded away into darkness and it was time for me to leave. Even though Jayson probably would not be home for another hour or two, I wanted to make sure I beat him home so that nothing looked unusual.

Before I left, Bret made me promise to meet him at the hotel on Friday. I agreed to do so, as long as he promised to keep our rendezvous secret.

I couldn't help but laugh out loud as I drove home. Finally, I felt like the old me... the Genevieve that didn't take shit from anything or anybody. Myeisha was right - I was starting to get all soft. I had let my guard down with Jayson and he had used it to his full advantage. Not anymore. The old Genevieve was back. If Jayson thought he could screw me over and get away with it, he was sadly mistaken. He could mess around with as many whores as he wanted to, but I would win in the end. If he ever tried to leave me, not only would I take half of his hard earned money, but I would also take his best friend away. He would never be able to open his own law firm without all of his money and help from Bret. I bet he couldn't top that!

I opened my front door and silence greeted me. I had made it home before Jayson, which meant I had time to change into my night clothes, climb into bed and act like everything was normal. I slipped my heels off my aching feet, reminding myself to buy another pair of gold heels but in three-inch instead on six. A flashback of Bret leaning me over the edge of the bed made me giggle out loud as I turned the knob to my bedroom door. The room was pitch black. I fumbled around, switching the fan off, then on twice before finally finding the light switch.

"Holy shit!" I shrieked as light flooded the room.

Jayson sat at the end of the bed. His lips were turned down in a grimace and his forehead was scrunched up and wrinkled. He wore an expression of intense anger mixed with concern.

"You scared the shit out of me Jayson! What are you doing sitting in the dark?" I asked, still trying to catch my breath.

"What are you doing is the question," Jayson boomed. The trace of concern that was just on his face waned. The look of disgust that replaced it made me shiver.

Had Bret went behind my back and called Jayson as soon as I left the hotel room? Maybe it had been a set-up, just like I had planned on setting Jayson up using Myeisha's friend, Candace. My heart was beating so fast that I could feel my body sway with each beat. I quickly debated whether I should make up a lie or confess and get it over with since he probably already knew the truth anyway.

"I got my hair done this morning, so I decided to get dressed up and go out with some friends," I said, settling on lying.

"If you were with friends, then why has Myeisha been leaving messages on the answering machine looking for you?" Jayson stood up pacing back and forth in front of me like he was cross-examining a witness.

"Because I wasn't with Myeisha. For your information, I went out with my hairdresser, Neeka, and some of her friends from the salon," I said, trying to maintain eye contact with him so that he would think I was being truthful. I brushed past him, walked over to my dresser and started removing my earrings and necklace as if the discussion was over.

"Then what the fuck is this!" he yelled, throwing a piece of paper on the floor by my foot.

I picked up the long slip of paper and flipped it over. Jayson had found the check for 2 million dollars that I had hid in my underwear drawer. I wanted to kick myself for not having chosen a better hiding spot, but I also couldn't believe Jayson had been searching through my personal belongings.

"What were you doing going through my stuff?" I asked sternly, turning around and glaring at him.

"I'm asking the questions right now and I want to know why you have a check for that amount of money and who is Jim McPherson?"

At a loss for words, I sat there staring at Jayson with a blank look. I was too embarrassed to tell him the truth about my mom's scam and how I had allowed her to drag me in on it. I stayed silent for what seemed like forever. There were so many lies between us now I wondered if the truth even mattered.

"Look, Gen. Tell me. Are you seeing this Jim guy? Is he paying you to sleep with him?" Jayson begged for answers.

"How dare you! You just basically called me a hig-priced prostitute," I yelled in disbelief.

"Well, that's exactly what it looks like to me!" he yelled back. "What else am I supposed to think when my wife has a large sum of money that she received from some man stuffed in her panty drawer!"

I had never seen him this mad before. He was still pacing and his hands were balled up into tight fists. I could tell that he had been crying before I walked in because his eyes were bloodshot red. He looked tired and worn down, like he had aged ten years in one day.

"Jayson, calm down. Jim McPherson is a friend of Mama Rose's. Well, he was a friend of Mama Rose's until he passed. We went to visit him at the hospital the day Mama Rose came to pick me up last week. He left me the money because he had a thing for Mama Rose back in the days and I guess he wished that I was his daughter. If you don't believe me, you can call Mama Rose and ask her."

I prayed that he wouldn't actually pick up the phone and call that woman. Lord knew she would never admit to her wrongdoings. There was no doubt that if Jayson asked her, Mama Rose would deny any involvement and throw me under the bus.

"If that's the case, then why didn't you tell me before now?"

"I didn't have a chance to. I just got it in the mail the other day and I wasn't planning on keeping it. I'm giving it to Mama Rose because I think that was his intention - for her to have it," I explained. I had mostly told the truth. I just failed to mention that Mama Rose had lied to Jim to make him think that I was his daughter and that I fully intended to keep the money.

He started to look calm like he was actually breathing again. He studied my face, looking for any sign that I was deceiving him. I walked over to him innocently pouting and said, "I would never cheat on you, Jayson. It makes me sad to think that you think I would do something that vile and disgusting."

"I didn't know what to think, Gen. All I know is that I couldn't bear to lose you."

Jayson hugged me and his tears fell onto my shoulder.

"You don't have to worry about losing me."

I laid my head on his familiar chest. The dresser mirror caught the image of us embracing. It reminded me of a picture we had taken at our wedding in the exact same pose. Except for our dress and the tears coming down Jayson's face, there wasn't much difference. Fighting back tears, I wondered how long I could keep up this charade and if our marriage would survive.

Chapter 15

The yellow, white and purple sign in front of Posh blinked off and on, illuminating the inside of Myeisha's compact car.

"Park over there near the rear of the building," I said, pointing to a dark and obscure spot toward the back of Posh. Expensive luxury cars with well-groomed men in business suits behind the wheels pulled into the parking lot. Business was starting to pick up and I didn't want to risk Jayson spotting us.

"Are you sure you want to be here?" Myeisha asked, driving to the back of the building where no one could see us. She had been trying to convince me all night to wait at home while she and Candace executed our plan. Maybe she thought I would react hysterically if my fears were confirmed. She probably envisioned me stabbing holes in his tire, throwing a brick through the window of his Navigator or worse, me assaulting him and getting us all locked up over the weekend. The truth was, I really didn't know how I would react if Jayson gave in to Candace's advances, but I was determined to stick around and see the outcome first-hand.

"Of course I'm sure. Would you please stop asking me?"

Candace shifted around in the back of the car. Leaning over the back of my seat, she popped her gum loudly in my ear.

"Girl, I know you are flipping out right now. I remember when I found out my ex-fiancé was cheating on me with my own sister. It felt like someone had just ripped my heart out and stomped on it. That's why I told Myeisha I had no problem helping y'all out for a small fee. Shoot, it's the least I can do," Candace said in her deep, southern drawl.

Candace seemed like a nice enough person. Nonetheless, her voice was outright annoying as nails on a chalkboard. Sure, she was physically attractive and what most people would call sexy, but she far from a natural beauty. Her rather average facial features were unimpressive, but her petite shapely figure made up for what her face lacked. Her small waist, long legs and curvaceous hips were obviously those of a dancer. However, her breasts that were way too cumbersome for her small frame were an obvious surgical upgrade. As a matter of fact, everything on her seemed to be artificially enhanced - her nails, eyelashes and even her waist-length hair weave. Jayson always told me how unappealing women with fake attributes was to him. I would be surprised if he even paid her any attention at all. I gritted my teeth and tossed her a fake grin.

"Yeah, thanks again," I said, now distracted by the silver Navigator pulling into Posh's valet. Jayson and two of his co-workers hopped out of the car. I was relieved to see Bret was not tagging along. Anytime Jayson spent away from Bret was less time he had to figure out what was going on between us. I had already been with Bret at the hotel two more times since our first encounter. Each time, I promised myself I would end things, only to end up back in bed with him a day or two later. Bret had even called me on my cellphone once when I was with Jayson. I had to pretend to be talking to Myeisha before quickly ending the call. Luckily, Jayson hadn't suspected anything. But, there was no telling when my luck would run out.

"Isn't that Jayson's car?" Myeisha asked, following my gaze.

"Yeah, but I think we should let him and his buddies get settled for a few minutes before we send Candace in," I suggested.

"Good idea!" Candace exclaimed. "Then, I can make my grand entrance." She flipped her long fake hair with the back of her hand and blew a big bubble of pink gum until it popped loudly in my ear again.

"I really think you should spit that out before you go in. I don't think Jayson would find that very attractive."

Myeisha caught on to the irritated tone of my voice and interjected.

"Yeah, Candace. Jayson is a bit bourgeois; he might think that's a turn-off and we want to give him as many chances as possible to prove how much of a dog he is," Myeisha explained to her.

"Okay, sure, I'll spit it out," she said.

We sat quietly for a few minutes before Candace asked, "Do you think they are settled now?"

I could tell she was anxious to get to work or maybe she just wanted to get away from me. She had been totally quiet since I had told her to stop popping her gum.

"Go ahead and do what you do best," I said.

"What do you mean by that?" Candace asked, defensively.

"I just mean go be sensual and enticing. Isn't that what you did for a living when you were a pole swinger?" I asked innocently.

"Come on you guys, this is crazy. We all talked about this before tonight. There should be no reason for all of this tension. Really, Gen are you sure you want to go through with this?" Myeisha asked, trying to mend things.

"I don't know what you're talking about Myeisha. I'm totally kosher." I turned up the volume on the radio. I wanted to block out Candace's annoying voice if she responded. Instead, Candace hopped out the car and headed to the front of the building. I watched as she strutted towards Posh. She walked with a twist in her hip and definite purpose, breaking her stride only to spit her wad of gum out on the pavement. The doorman opened the door for her and she disappeared inside.

"I know you told me not to ask anymore, but I really need to know that you are okay with all of this Gen," Myeisha said, placing her hand on my shoulder.

I knew Myeisha only wanted to make sure I was okay. She was my best friend and the only person that I felt I could truly count on.

"I'm fine, Myeisha. Besides, I already know Jayson won't give Candace the time of day."

At least, that's what I wanted to believe.

Chapter 16

Time went by slowly as we waited for Candace to come out. The flickering lights from the sign at Posh were starting to give me a migraine. The fact that I had eaten a whole pack of jelly beans that Myeisha fished out of her purse was not doing much for my stomach either. It had been over an hour since Candace had strutted into the bar. Several other women that ranked as skank material had also entered the bar since then. From the looks of the women that were disappearing inside, it was safe to say that Posh wasn't so posh after all.

"Oh my gosh, duck!" Myeisha screamed, sliding all the way down in her seat. I instinctively followed her lead and slid down, too.

"What are we hiding from?" I asked.

"Candace just walked out with some guy. I think it's Jayson." Myeisha stated, hesitantly.

"Let me see!" I exclaimed, peeking out of the window.

Myeisha scooted close to me and leaned over my lap to get a closer look. Our breath fogged up the window as we strained to see who Candace was walking out with.

Candace switched her hips provocatively as her male escort followed behind her, his head looking down at her ass the whole time. I reached for the door handle. I was so hot, I could feel steam coming from every pore in my body.

"Wait!" Myeisha yelled.

She pushed my hand away from the door handle. Myeisha was my girl, but she was inches from getting clocked. I was on a mission to rip Jayson's head off of his shoulders and no one including my beloved best-friend was going to stop me.

"Watch out, Myeisha," I stated gruffly. I tried to peel her hands from the door handle, but she used every bit of strength her small frame could muster up to keep me trapped inside her car.

"Stop, you're acting like a psychopath! What are you going to do, beat him up and cause a scene?"

"Yeah and you and the entire United States Army ain't going to do nothing about it," I said, overpowering her and grabbing the door handle. I flung the car door open with force. I marched across the parking lot. Myeisha's pleading faded into the background. I couldn't believe my husband was talking to a low-class, backwoods tramp in front of the same people we attended Christmas and charity fund-raising parties with. I would be the first to admit I wasn't an angel. Sleeping with Bret wasn't something that I was exactly proud of, but at least I had the decency to do my dirt behind closed doors.

I walked up behind Jayson, tapped him on his shoulder and before he could turn all the way around, I punched him in the side of his head as hard as I could. The impact of his cheekbone against my knuckles made me wince in pain.

"Damn it," I yelled, shaking my right hand.

"What did you do that for!?" Candace shouted, looking appalled. Her mouth was hanging open as if her jaw had become unhinged.

"Because that's how I roll, bitch," I said, calmly squeezing my hand to make sure I still had feeling in it.

"But, that's not you husband. It's just some guy I just met," Candace exclaimed.

For the first time, I actually really looked closely at the man I had just hit; the man who had dropped to his knees on the pavement and was holding his cheek with the palm of his hand. Candace was right. It wasn't my husband. He had the same low hair-cut, well-groomed beard and almond complexion as Jayson. They were even very similar in height and weight, but it wasn't him. I had overreacted and mistaken this poor guy for Jayson.

Myeisha pulled up next to us in her car.

"Get in!" she hollered out the window. Candace and I both stared at her blankly. We were both in shock from the unexpected turn of events.

"I said, get in the fucking car, both of you!" Myeisha repeated at the top of her lungs. John Doe was beginning to recover. He stood up, shaking his head back and forth. He was coming out of his daze, which only gave us a few more seconds to get the hell out of Dodge. We piled in the car as quickly as possible. Somehow, I ended up in the backseat and Candace ended up shotgun. Myeisha peeled out of the parking light like she was leaving the scene of a crime. Which in all reality, she was. The smell of burnt rubber filled the air.

"I knew it was a bad idea for you to come along," Myeisha moaned, rubbing her head.

"Well, I thought it was Jayson. All those men in business suits coming in and out of Posh… well, they all started to look alike. Then, I saw him coming out with Candace, so I assumed it was Jayson. Even you thought it was Jayson, Myeisha."

"Yeah, but I didn't tell you to go sucker-punch him," Myeisha snapped. She kept checking the rearview mirror as if she expected the police to pull us over at any moment.

Candace remained quiet in the front seat. She looked sullen, as if she had just lost her favorite pet.

"What's the matter, Candace?" Myeisha asked.

"Nothing, other than the fact that your friend just totally ruined my night. That guy she assaulted owned his own law firm here in Vegas. He drives a Ferrari and has a vacation house in Italy. He even offered to fly me out there this summer. We were just about to exchange numbers when one flew over the cuckoo's nest." Candace looked over her shoulder and gave me the evil eye.

"Well, you were supposed to be trying to get with Jayson, not with other random guys," I replied, rolling my eyes.

"Jayson didn't pay me any attention, even after I came on to him twice. He told me he was married. What was I supposed to do, waste the rest of my night? Hell no! Not with all those fine ass, rich men in there."

"He really told you that he was married?" I asked Candace.

"Yes, but you are still going to pay me, right?"

"Yeah, sure," I mumbled. I thought knowing that Jayson had turned Candace's advances down would have made me the happiest person on earth, but instead I felt horrible. All the time I was suspecting Jayson of being a cheater, he was actually being a faithful husband.

My own fears and insecurities had led me to doubt my husband and betray our marriage. I would have felt better if I could have walked away with some excuse for my recent behavior, for someone to blame for my sneaking around with my husband's best friend. Now, I was left with nothing but raw guilt for my actions and it stung like hell.

Chapter 17

"If that's how you want to spend your portion of the money - on some old crazy fool that claims they can read the future - then you go right on ahead. I'm going to the mall. Macy's is having a shoe sale and you aren't going to make me miss it on account of all this voodoo nonsense," I told Mama Rose.

"Nonsense?!" Mama Rose shrieked. "If you believe in the Spirit of the Holy Ghost like I raised you to, then you have gotta believe in all spirits - good or bad. These dreams I keep having is something awful, Genevieve, and I need to know what they mean."

I had decided to cash the check from poor Mr. McPherson and spilt it with Mama Rose, since it was her idea in the first place. I had already booked a European wine excursion with my newly acquired fortune. In six months, me and Jayson would be would be off exploring vineyards overseas. I thought it would be a great way for us to start fresh together.

"I said I'm not going to see some old hex lady and that's that."

All I wanted to do was have a little fun shopping and building my wardrobe for the trip. All Mama Rose seemed intent on doing was ruining my day. I had hoped that when I gave her the money, she would disappear for a while. Maybe take one of her smooth-talking cat daddies that she kept hidden away or maybe even one of her god-fearing church sisters with her on a trip to China, or somewhere else far away. But instead, she wanted to take me with her to the psychic up the street. Go figure.

"When you ignore these kinda messages, bad things can happen. This here ain't nothing to play around with," Mama Rose cautioned. "And you in every one of my dreams, Gen. That's why I think you should go with me."

I was now regretting letting Mama Rose drive to the bank to deposit the check into my secret separate account. It meant I had no other means of transportation. I could argue, but in the end, there was no saying no to Mama Rose. If she wanted to go to see some witch lady, there was nothing I could do about it other than sit back and enjoy the ride.

"Okay, fine, as long as we make it to Macy's by noon," I compromised.

The chime went off as we entered the dim storefront. Whoever was supposed to be alerted by the ring was apparently busy because no one appeared to greet us. A light from a separate room in the back of the store was the only indication that the store was even open. Even though it was broad daylight outside, purple curtains hung from the window and ceiling throughout the store, voiding out most of the sun. The aroma of frankincense and myrrh filled the room. A gigantic black and white sign reading, **Welcome all Seekers,** was on the wall behind the register.

"Are you sure anyone is even here? Maybe we should come back later," I said, eager to escape the uneasy feeling I had in the pit of my stomach.

"She's here. I called earlier. She's expecting us."

Flickering candles lined the walls. A large display case filled with everything from a shrunken head, crystals and protection pendants to books on the power of healing aligned the wall behind the register. Even Mama Rose looked a little spooked by the mystical surroundings.

"Well, maybe you need to ring that bell over there and let her know we are here," I said, pointing to shiny silver bell positioned on top of an old fashioned mahogany desk.

"You don't have to ring no bell. I know when I have company," a hoarse voice with a deep Louisiana twang announced.

From her voice alone, I expected to see some old hunchback cackling hen on a cane stumbling from the backroom. I was shocked to see a beautiful, middle-aged lady with smooth, caramel skin and bright, round, piercing eyes appear. She was a far cry from Dionne Warwick or anyone from the Psychic Friends Network that I had ever seen. This lady could give Naomi Campbell a run for her money.

"There's no way I could miss either one of ya'. Yawl's auras are so strong, they entered the room long before you did."

She stood with her hand resting on the edge of the wooden counter, staring at me and Momma Rose. Her alarmingly stunning and unusual, silver eyes held us captivated in our spots.

"Well, don't just sit there staring at me, have a seat," she said, motioning to several plush, colorful pillows placed in a circle on the floor.

I felt embarrassed for staring at her, but her rare attractiveness was something to be admired and quite compelling.

"I do apologize, but I am sure you have already been told how beautiful you are, especially your eyes," I said, trying to explain myself.

"Too bad they're not of much use," she said in her unfitting, croaky voice. "I've been blind as a bat since I was three years old. My mother always told me it was the price I had to pay for having the sight to see what others can't."

I wanted to kick myself for not realizing how she felt her way around the room and to her seat on the floor across from me and Mama Rose, but even with her telling us, it was hard to believe that she was blind. There was no emptiness in her eyes when she looked at me. It felt like not only could she see me, but she could look so deep inside me that all my vulnerabilities were left totally exposed.

"Thank you for seeing us today, Madeline. You came highly recommended from a friend of mine. I'm Rose and this is my daughter, Genevieve, right here. She's who I'm really concerned about. I've been having some dreams lately that I don't know how to make sense of." Mama Rose was staring at Madeline with the same amazement that I was.

"Well, I don't see everybody. I'm not much for the normal questions most folks have like, 'When am I going to meet the love of my life?' 'Am I ever going to get married?' 'Will I get a promotion at work?' All those things are so trivial. I much prefer a challenge."

Madeline smiled and adjusted her feet beneath her. There was something warm and comforting about her. She seemed just as fascinated about meeting us as we were about meeting her.

"So, let's start," she said, extending her hands out to us. Mama Rose grasped one hand while I held the other. Her skin was just as soft as it appeared to be. Madeline concentrated on something beyond the physical and beyond anything me or Mama Rose could understand. Everything in the room seemed to shift suddenly. The shadows, the purple drapes and the flickering flames all shuddered. A cool draft blew through the room. I looked over at Mama Rose for reassurance, but she was still staring captivatingly at Madeline.

"I'm concerned about both of you and the people around you," Madeline whispered. Her relaxed manner quickly turned tense.

Mama Rose looked at me and threw a quick "I told you so..." glance my way.

"I am doing your readings together because you two are so much alike that your paths are intertwining. If you don't start making the right choices, history will repeat itself," she said, letting go of Mama Rose's hand and grabbing my other free hand in hers. Her warning was obviously directed at me.

"What do you mean, history will repeat itself?" I asked, wondering whether or not I wanted to hear the real answer.

The worst thing that had ever happened to me was when I had served time in jail. It had been the longest 60 days of my life and something I never wanted to relive. The state's defense attorney that was originally appointed to my case was so inept that I had only seen her once in my first thirty days there. The possibility of spending my entire life behind those dingy concrete walls and steel gates seemed like an absolute surety until Jayson was introduced to me as my new attorney. When my mother hired Jayson, he came to see me every day. That was when I finally felt some hope of being a free woman again. Within weeks, Jayson had all my charges dropped. There had been so many accidents at that intersection that the city didn't want to bring any attention to the case in fear that they might be found negligent themselves. Jayson used that fear against them to exonerate me. The new pedestrian crosswalk at that intersection reminded me of the accident every time I passed by.

"In order for this all to end and have any good come from it, you have to face the truth," Madeline said.

"I don't know what you are talking about," I said, pushing thoughts from my past as far back as I could.

"I've never seen a veil as dark and heavy as the one you and your mother use to hide your secrets and your past. You are both gifted in your own rights. You are both able to hide your secrets from even me. However, I can't help you if you are not willing to be honest with yourselves."

"Well, I didn't ask for help! This was all my mother's crazy idea!" I shouted, pulling my hand away from hers and standing up.

"Please don't leave," Madeline begged. "If you don't listen to me, someone very near to you will die."

I stumbled backwards, trying to get away from Madeline as fast as I could. Mama Rose was getting up from her position on the floor, but not fast enough for me; I was already heading out of the door. I stood outside, waiting for Mama Rose to come out and open the car. I cursed under my breath, disappointed that I had let Mama Rose talk me into another fiasco.

"Can you believe what that crazy woman said?" I asked Mama Rose as we drove home. She had been quiet ever since we had left the store. Now, she was acting as if she was too busy concentrating on traffic to answer me.

"I mean, you don't just go around telling people someone is going to die. She's more like a psycho, not a psychic! It's obvious that she doesn't know what she talking about. I don't have any deep dark secrets and neither do you. Right, Mama Rose?"

Mama Rose sucked her teeth before responding. "Well, baby, everybody has a skeleton or two in their closet."

Chapter 18

Madeline's knowing eyes and eerie warning filled my dreams night after night. I wanted to believe that it was just a bunch of superstitious mumbo-jumbo, but truth be told, I couldn't shake the uneasiness I had been feeling since the moment I stepped in her storefront. I tossed, turned and sweated in my sleep so much that Jayson had suggested that I go see a doctor. He had no clue about me going to see a psychic or about the warning that I had received. If he did know, he would just tell me to shake it off. Jayson operated on pure black and white facts. If he couldn't prove it, he didn't believe it.

"Are you having dreams about the accident again?" Jayson asked, rubbing sleep from his eyes.

It was two o'clock in the morning and the third time I had gotten up to get a drink of water. The sheets were soaked with my perspiration and my night sweats were keeping us both awake.

"What accident?"

I grabbed the remote, turned on the television and flipped to some late night infomercial. I wasn't really watching the lady dice a tomato with a state-of-the-art stainless steel vegetable slicer, but I was allowing her monotone pitch to lull me into a semi-trance.

"The one that resulted in a man lying in a coma at the county hospital, Gen. I know we haven't talked about it in a while, but even though the accident wasn't your fault, you never, not once, asked me how the victim is doing."

"Look, Jayson, I'm really tired right now. Besides, I already know how he's doing. He is on a feeding tube in a coma at University Medical Center. When and if he ever comes out of the coma, I assume there will be a news story on it, or you'll give me an update."

I waved the remote and started channel surfing. Jayson was starting to annoy me. Here he was, trying to debate with me about how guilty I should feel about a horrible freak accident. It was as if he expected me to punish myself for something that I had already learned to live with.

"Wow, that's really cold. I didn't expect that from you."

"Really?" I asked, setting the remote down and glaring at him. "Well, what exactly did you expect Jayson? You're acting like I purposely hit him. He's the one who walked out in front of my car. If he had been paying attention, then I wouldn't have had to spend sixty days of my life locked up in a cell with some bitch named Sheniqua. He's not the only victim in this situation."

"I'm not accusing you of anything, Genevieve. I'm just trying to figure out what going on. I've noticed that you've been on edge lately. You haven't been getting more than a few hours of sleep for the past few nights."

"I'm sorry," I said, turning and batting my eyes at him.

"You're right, I haven't been myself lately. I'm probably just restless. Other than shopping and shooting the breeze with Myeisha, I haven't been all that productive. I was thinking maybe I should get back into my volunteer work. I miss working with women at the shelter."

I had worked as a part-time volunteer at a shelter for women who were victims of domestic violence off and on for the last year. It had helped to preoccupy myself whenever Jayson was committed to a difficult case and putting in extra hours at the office, like he was now. I had planned on returning to college and finishing up my last year of schooling needed to complete my Masters in Psychology, but right now just wasn't the right time.

"I think that's a great idea. I know helping those women really made you feel good," Jayson said, walking into our closet and throwing on a robe.

"I'll contact the director, Ms. Mansfield, on Monday. I'm sure they could use all the help they could get."

I jotted a reminder note down on a piece of scrap paper from our night stand to call the shelter.

"Since it seems like neither one of us are going to get much sleep tonight, I'm going to make a pot of coffee. Would you like a cup?" Jayson offered, sliding on his house shoes.

"Thanks, I'll take mine black," I replied.

Jayson scooted out into the dark hall. I heard him bump into a wall and swear before I the familiar click of the light switch came.

"You okay out there?" I giggled.

"Yeah, but remind me install a light with a motion sensor in the hallway before one us falls down the stairs and breaks our neck one night."

I felt bad for jumping down his throat just now. Even though he was still working on the same difficult case at work, he had made it home on time for dinner almost every day this week. He was really trying hard to make more time for me. I was also making an honest effort to be a good wife in return. I hadn't seen Bret in over a week now.

ZZZZZZZZ.....ZZZZZZZ. I climbed out of bed to follow the low buzz of my cell phone. The sound led me to my purse that was sitting on the counter in my bathroom. Once again, I had forgotten to take my phone out of my purse and put it on the charger. I dug through my miniature suitcase-sized handbag and pulled out a set of keys, a bottle of lotion and tube of lipstick before finding my phone. I was preparing myself to hear one of Myeisha's sexcapade stories when I recognized the phone number on the screen.

"Bret, what are you doing calling me right now? Jayson is here," I whispered, expecting to hear Jayson's footsteps coming up the staircase at any moment.

"You haven't stopped by to see me or returned any of my messages lately, so I thought this might get your attention," Bret breathed into the phone. He sounded agitated, but just as awake as I was.

"You know my situation, Bret," I said, softly shutting the bathroom door behind me and turning on the faucet to mute my voice in case Jayson returned.

"And you know mine. I need to see you today, so you need to find a way to break away from the little hubby."

"I can't today. We already have plans," I lied. It was Sunday and Jayson and I had no plans, other than to catch up on our sleep and maybe watch the cooking channel in between our naps.

"If you're that busy, then I guess I'll just have to stop by and visit my best friend and his wife. It would be nice for all of us to hang out together. You know, catch up on things. Jayson and I haven't really seen each other that much at work since they assigned me to a new case. It would be nice to chat with him," Bret stated menacingly.

A sudden loud knock on the bathroom door nearly made me jump out of my skin.

"Gen, are you okay in there? I heard the water running downstairs. Are you taking a shower?" Jayson yelled through the door.

"Umm...no. I'm just freshening up. I'll be out in second," I yelled back over the splashing water.

"Okay, honey. I made your coffee black, just like you like it. I'll leave it on your nightstand," he said. I could hear the clatter of the porcelain saucer on my nightstand.

"Thanks."

"Isn't that sweet? Jayson made you some coffee. Too bad he got your order all wrong. Next time, tell him you like your coffee with cream," Bret laughed before hanging the phone up in my face.

Chapter 19

It was a combination of the psychic's warning and Jayson's comment the other night that lead me to the fifth floor of the county hospital. The entire building had been recently renovated and looked remarkably different from the grimy and slightly dilapidated interior I remembered.

"May I help you?" A chunky, red-headed, freckle-faced male nurse asked. He was carrying a clipboard in one hand and balancing a metal try with a long sharp needle in the other.

"I'm looking for room 520," I said, barely able to remove my eyes from the horrific looking instrument on the tray.

"You're headed the right way. Just keep straight and turn at the end of the corridor," the nurse replied, never slowing his pace or cracking a smile.

At that moment, I considered turning around and heading back to the parking lot. The freshly painted walls and tastefully chosen artwork that lined the hallway was a failed attempt to make this place more cheerful. In the designer's defense, there wasn't much one could do to make this place not reek of sickness and death.

I couldn't turn back now. I was on a mission to make things right in my life once again. I couldn't continue walking around with an impending cloud of doom looming over me, waiting with bated breath for someone near to me to drop dead like a fly at any given moment. The man in room 520 was the only skeleton I had in my closet. I had tried to erase him and the accident from my memory. After meeting Jayson, forgetting everything that had happened had been so easy. But occasionally, the memories would come and go. I guess I really didn't need a psychic to tell me that the past would come back to haunt me. However, she was wrong about one thing: I was nothing like my mother. Mama Rose would never have apologized for anything she had ever done wrong. I, on the other hand, was ready to admit my faults and wrongdoings. I planned on apologizing to Professor Donovan, even if he was in a coma and could not hear me. My conscience told me that I at least owed him an apology for trying to kill him. But my mind told me that I didn't owe him a damn thing and he got exactly what he deserved.

After a two-year affair with my English Professor, he had promised to leave his wife of ten years to be with me. I had kept my end of the bargain by keeping our relationship under wraps. None of his colleagues, nor any of the students at the college knew we were seeing each other. I had even hidden our affair from Myeisha. The only promise he kept was giving me an A in his course. On the last day of the spring semester, I spotted him walking down the hallway with a young Asian girl that I had had as a classmate in my Psychology class the previous semester. She was laughing at something he had just said and she looked up at him, endearingly. It was the same look I always gave him. When he walked past me without so much as a nod of acknowledgement, I knew he had no intention of leaving his wife or even continuing our affair. He had found a new object of affection. I hadn't planned for things to turn out the way they did, but after I followed him from the same hotel he always took me and saw him walking across the street, it seemed like an opportune moment and I seized it. I wasn't in a fit of rage like most people claim to be when they try to take someone out. I felt calm, clear and convinced, convinced that everything my mother had told me about men being untrustworthy, cheating, selfish bastards had been right all along. Since no one knew our connection, it had been easy to pitch the story that he was just some random pedestrian. Without his side of the story, there was no opposition.

If I had to do it all again, I probably would have made a different decision. Not because I felt sorry for Professor Donovan or his wife and two children. If his wife knew what he had been doing behind her back, she wouldn't feel sorry for him either. But, I would do it over again to avoid the chances of having this awful secret exposed. What would my family, friends and Jayson think if they knew the truth? I worried every day that Professor Donovan would come out of his coma and that he would remember seeing my face right before my car plowed into him. If he didn't remember that, he would certainly remember my name once someone told him who hit him. It had come up that I was a student of his, but it was taken for nothing more than a mere coincidence. I had always lived on the hope that his family would give up and pull the plug, but that never happened. I guess his wife really loved him, which is a shame, considering he probably fucked half the female student body on campus.

"Excuse me, ma'am. You need to check in before you can visit any of patients on this floor," an uptight, elderly woman with a volunteer badge grumbled from behind a desk. She was using her pen to point at a red binder, which apparently was the sign-in log.

"What floor is this?" I asked, looking around and acting confused.

"You're on the fifth floor, the intensive care unit," the old woman said, shaking her head in disbelief of my ignorance and pointing to a sign in front of me that clearly read 5th Floor, ICU.

"Oh my gosh, I'm sorry. I was in such a rush to get to the bathroom that I got off on the wrong floor. Is there a bathroom on this level that I can use?" I asked, shifting back on forth as if the will to hold my urine was dissipating as we spoke.

"Normally, we only let authorized visitors use the restroom on this level, but if you really have to go, there's a bathroom at the end of the hallway."

"Thank you!"

I walked down the hallway with an air of urgency. I jetted down the corridor before she could change her mind.

Her beady, little eyes followed me all the way to the end of the hallway until I entered the restroom. *Just my luck to have Florence Nightingale reincarnated on his watch*, I thought. The bathroom reeked of lemon Lysol and the lingering stench of someone's discarded bowel movement. I held my breath and fought the compulsion to vomit. I reconsidered my plans. I had told Jayson that I called the shelter early and that they needed my help immediately. I had to find a way to see Bret before he blew a fuse, but I also needed to put my woes to rest. As much as I wanted to turn back now, I needed to see Professor Donovan. I felt doing so would appease my guilty conscious and stop

Madeline's warning from coming true. I poked my head out of the restroom, gulping in huge swallow of fresh air. Nurse Nightingale was busy helping another visitor sign into her trusty red binder.

I tip-toed quietly along the floor, making sure my heels did not clack against the tile and ducked into room 520. Professor Michael Donovan, or "Mickey" as I affectionately had called him, had so many tubes and machines attached to him that I barely recognized him. The steady rhythm of the respirator and a low, constant beeping from one of the machines was the only noise in the room.

I had a vision of our last night together. He had surprised me and taken me to his vacation home in the mountains. We had lobster, shrimp and a bottle of wine over candlelight. That was the night he had promised to leave his wife. I couldn't figure out why he made that promise, knowing he had another mistress on the side. Maybe he was planning to leave his wife, just not for me. The machines beeped and wheezed and I pondered how easy it would be to silence them… to silence him. Fresh lilacs and helium balloons sat on a small table next to his bed.

"I'm sorry, please forgive me," I whispered, leaning over and kissing him on his cheek in the only space void of tape and tubes. I hadn't expected tears to flow, but I had thought I would have some type of emotion – regret, pain or perhaps loathing. Instead, I felt like I was looking at a complete stranger. There was no feeling at all, other than the hope that I was being saved from impending doom and my night sweats would end. I snuck out of the room and back down the hallway.

"Thanks," I said, tossing Florence Nightingale a fake smile as I walked past her.

"Mmm hmm," she mumbled, barely looking up at me. I hopped on the elevator and pushed L for Lobby. Already, I was feeling on top of the world. I felt assured that my magical kiss had made amends and that, although he was in the deepest of sleeps, Professor Donovan had forgiven me in some way and that meant Madeline's warning was null and void. If he couldn't forgive me for hitting him, then I would at least be blessed for being so kind as not to pull the plug from the machine that kept him alive when I had just had ample opportunity to do so. With one burden lifted, I was ready to tackle my next obstacle: getting Bret off my back. But, that was easy. Bret was a sucker for a blow job and I had nothing better to do on a Sunday afternoon.

Chapter 20

The last time I had seen Bret, he had talked me into allowing him to take me out to dinner. I didn't think it was a good idea to be seen in public together. If one of Jayson's associates or his mother, who lived here in town, saw us together, things could easily get ugly. I wasn't afraid we would run into Jayson. A new lead on his case had developed, so he had spent the night at the office, pouring over evidence with another colleague. He had called me early this morning to let me know that he wouldn't be at home until well after dinner today. I had agreed to dinner under one condition: We go to a restaurant on the other side of town.

"Where are you headed off to?" Myeisha asked. She had called me just as I was pulling out of my driveway on the way to meet Bret at Geisha, a five-star Japanese restaurant.

"Nowhere important," I mumbled, evasively. I was glad she was not sitting next to me; my red cheeks would have given me away.

"You've been going 'nowhere important' a lot lately. Sounds to me like you got another brother on the side, handling business."

Myeisha's observation was pretty dead-on, but I wasn't ready to admit it.

"I'm not cheating on Jayson. What type of woman do you think I am?"

"A woman that likes a nice, long, hard one in her just like any other woman does. You don't have to act all high sadity with me. I wouldn't blame you if you were getting a little action on the side. Shoot, Jayson is always away *at* work when he needs to be puttin' in some work at home. If a man ain't taking care of his woman, he gotta know another brother will."

"Well, for your information, Jayson and I are doing just fine in that area. I don't need any additional assistance."

I really wanted to be able to share everything with Myeisha. I wanted to tell her how right she was and how Bret knew how to hit it so good, he had me speaking in tongues and hollering out his name. But, Myeisha wasn't the type of person that could hold a secret, even if her life depended on it. That's why everyone at the beauty parlor knew all her business in the first place. If I told Myeisha about Bret, everyone from the shampoo girl at Oh So Natural to Mama Rose would know by noon tomorrow. I knew she really didn't mean any harm when she ran her mouth; it was just part of her nature.

"Even though *you* are not sharing today, I do have something to share with you," Myeisha announced, with an air of mystery.

"What, lap dances are buy one get one half off this weekend?"

"Ha, ha. Very funny. Actually, it's much better than that. Troy is back."

I couldn't believe what I was hearing. Myeisha was announcing that Troy was back like she was announcing Santa Claus was coming to town. The giddiness in her voice was nauseating. Troy was the only man on earth that Myeisha had ever fallen in love with. He was also the only man that had beaten her ass so bad, she had to be hospitalized.

"You mean, they let that asshole out of prison?" I asked, with disgust.

"Well, they had to. He only got a year. They gave him time off his sentence for good behavior, so they let him out last week. And, by the way, he was in jail, not prison."

Now, I really couldn't believe my own ears. I took the phone away from my ear and looked at it like it was a two-headed, purple monster. I returned my focus back to the road and took a deep breath. I understood from dealing with the women at the shelter that talking to a battered woman required a delicate balance between patience and firmness.

"Myeisha, I don't understand how you can be so excited about someone who gave you two black eyes and broken ribs. Remember you had to stay in the hospital three nights because you had a concussion and they needed to monitor you."

There was a long silence before she responded. For a moment, I thought she had actually hung up.

"I know, but he's the father of my child," she whispered with sadness in her voice.

I was about to touch on a very sensitive subject. Myeisha had gotten pregnant by Troy during their two-year relationship. Four months into the pregnancy, Myeisha had a miscarriage. I suspected the lost was directly related to the physical abuse she was suffering. She was so devastated that I don't think she ever came to terms with it. I was in jail at the time, fighting my case. I always regretted not being able to be there for her during one of the most difficult times of her life.

"Technically, you didn't have a child with him and even if you did, that does not mean you have to be subjected to his abuse," I responded.

After I said it, I wanted to retract the first part of my statement. I knew in her heart she felt like her child was as real and special as any other child, whether it had made it into the world or not.

"I'm sorry. I didn't mean it like that," I quickly said, wishing I had thought before speaking.

"It's okay. I know you didn't mean it like that. I just thought you would be happy for me. I went to counseling after all of that and Troy went to anger management counseling in jail, even though he was only in there for robbery. He showed me the certificate today. I believe in second chances."

Myeisha was trying her best to convince me that Troy wouldn't put his hands on her again, but I knew better.

"I'm glad he went to counseling, Myeisha, but I don't think there's enough counseling in the world to help that man. He is pure evil. Don't you remember how he tried to convince you to take money from your job at the bank? If you were actually dumb enough to listen to him, you'd probably be in prison right now. Oh, and don't forget when he spray painted your car because he thought you were cheating on him."

Myeisha's cousin, Allen, had come to visit Myeisha from out of town. She was in the shower, getting ready to pick Allen up from the airport when Troy came home and saw a note next to the phone that said 'Pick Allen up from the airport at 5'. Instead of asking Myeisha what the note was about, he went in her storage closet, found a can of paint and spray painted her car - all while she was taking a shower. Myeisha had to drive to the airport and pick up her cousin with "Dirty Slut" written across both sides of her car in hot pink.

"Of course I remember. Do you think I'll ever forget anything he's done to me? I just decided that I forgive him. Nobody's perfect. I love him and I want to give us a second chance."

I could tell there was no convincing her otherwise at this point. He was her one point of weakness. There was no question about it, Myeisha would regret her decision to take Troy back and I would be there to pick up the pieces when it happened.

Chapter 21

"Guess who's going to be opening their own law firm," Bret stated with vigor. He held up a glass flute filled with Cristal, in the air.

"Are you serious!? Congratulations!" I shrieked excitedly as we clanked our glasses together.

When I had arrived at Geisha, I was relieved to see there were no more than five or six other groups of patrons in the restaurant, most of whom appeared to be businessmen. I was even more relieved when the waiter sat us in a dark cozy table in the rear of the expansive room. The restaurant's atmosphere was secluded, but chic - the type of place a white-collared CEO would take a potential Asian investor that he's trying to impress.

"I'm really happy for you, but I thought you and Jayson had always planned on opening a firm together," I said, hoping the mention of Jayson's name would not open Pandora's Box.

"Things change, Genevieve. I'll give credit where credit's due: Jayson is good at what he does. I could definitely see him making partner one day at Franklin and Franklin, but I could never picture him owning his own firm."

"And why not?" I asked trying not to sound too defensive because, after all, he was speaking of my husband.

"Because he's a policy and rule follower and I'm a policy and rule maker. That's the difference between him and me. I don't limit myself by staying within society's standards and expectations; I challenge them. Jayson's a good ole' boy; he never colors outside of the lines. I prefer to doodle outside the lines as much as possible and create new concepts."

I didn't agree with Bret, but I wasn't going to argue with him. Jayson was one of the best defense attorneys in Las Vegas. Because of his record and expertise, he often got chosen to take on the most challenging cases, like the one he was working on now. I was beginning to think that Bret was more than a little jealous of Jayson. It was obvious that our affair definitely attributed to his jealousy, but I wondered if Bret had been resentful of Jayson's success all along.

"I think Jayson would be really hurt if you opened a firm and excluded him. He told me you guys have been planning on doing this since you were in college," I said, trying to reason with him.

"I could think of worse things that would hurt Jayson more than me opening a law firm without him," Bret stated with the crookedness of a slimy car salesman.

Our date and this conversation were going nowhere fast. I knew all of my improprieties would catch up with me sooner or later. I had gotten myself into a lot of jams over the years and had always been able to somehow walk away clean, but getting rid of Bret wasn't going to be as easy.

"If it is capital you need, Jayson has some money stashed away. He could really help you get things up and going."

I was thinking of the million dollars I had gotten from Mama Rose's scheme. I would be more than willing to give Jayson the money to help him and Bret start a firm. All I wanted was for Bret and Jayson's relationship to be the same as it was before the affair. Now, Bret rarely called Jayson or came to the house to visit anymore. One day, while Jayson and I shared an omelet and coffee at breakfast, *he* had even mentioned that Bret seemed more distant.

"I don't want anything from Jayson, except for one thing," Bret moaned, reaching across the table to hold my hand. The back of his hand bumped into my champagne glass, spilling the contents onto my lap. A puddle of Cristal soaked through my skirt and eased its way up my thigh. I hopped up from the table to stop it from flowing into my underwear.

"I'm sorry, Genevieve," Bret stammered. He had gotten up from the table and dabbed at my just-below-the–knee fitted black skirt with his napkin.

"It's black, it's won't stain," I reassured him.

"But you must feel uncomfortable. Why don't you go freshen up in ladies room? I believe it's over there."

"Okay, I'll be right back," I said, heading across the room.

A couple of the businessmen eyed me as I walked past. They whispered to each other in a foreign language that I assumed was Japanese. I didn't understand what they were saying, but their lustful stares explained it all. Feeling like a main course at dinner, I lowered my eyes and quickened my pace towards the restroom.

"To one year," I heard a familiar male's voice say.

I stopped dead in my tracks like a hunting dog on alert. Following the sound of the voice, I turned around and stared at a couple several tables away. They were occupied, completing their celebration cheer, so they didn't notice me watching them from afar. I could tell that the lady, even though she was seated, was much taller than me. Her thin, narrow face was elegant and beautiful. She swung her fake, breast-length weave across her shoulder, giggling and flirting with her companion. The man reached across the table, cupping her chin in his hand. The gleam in the eyes that I knew so well clearly let me know they were in love. I wanted to regurgitate my sushi all of the plush, red carpet of Geisha. I wanted to walk over to the table, rip the weave off the lady's head and shove it down my husband's throat until he slowly stopped breathing.

But I couldn't make a scene. If I did, then the plan that was developing in my head was at risk of being exposed. I held back screaming at the top of my lungs, falling out on the floor and throwing a fit like a four-year-old who just got their favorite blankie taken from them. Instead, I turned around, walked back to the table and politely told Bret that I wanted to leave - right now. Surprisingly, he didn't ask any questions. Maybe the look on my face - like I was ready to murder - was what caused him to not pressure me for answers. He paid the bill and we left unnoticed. I don't know if Bret had seen Jayson or not. If he did, he didn't say anything to me.

"To a year."

The phrase repeated in my head over and over while we drove to Bret's. What did Jayson mean when he said that to her? A year of what? If Jayson had been seeing another woman for a year, it would explain a lot of things. It would also give me a reason to not feel guilty for doing what I was about to do. My head was swimming with a million crazy thoughts. I couldn't talk to Bret and Myeisha had her own problems. Besides, there was only one person that I knew that could put a dog in his place: Mama Rose.

Chapter 22

"I knew it! I knew it! I knew it! That son of a bitch!"

I had just told Mama Rose what I had seen and heard at the restaurant yesterday. It would be an understatement to say that she was not pleased with the situation. The fact that I had come to her house meant that I was desperate for help. It was the first time in over six months that I had stepped foot in Mama Rose's home. Being on her territory was almost as frightening as walking into the den of a lion. In public, she was nothing nice, but if you pissed her off or disrespected her in the confines of her own home, you were taking the risk of losing your life or a limb. It was just as I remembered: neat and tidy. Everything had a place and was painstakingly organized. The dishes were color-coordinated and stacked from largest to smallest. The silver spoon she handed me to stir my tea had been polished to a mirror-like finish. I could see my tired, grief-stricken face staring back at me in its reflection. A framed photo of me and Georgette when we were teenagers hung on the wall above the kitchen table. I recalled how Mama Rose had forced us both to wear the hideous, flower-patterned dresses that we had on in the picture. Our smiles were forced and our expressions sullen.

"And what kind of dirty whore would lay up with another woman's husband? She must be one those prostitutes or strippers. You better go see a doctor and get yourself checked down there. No telling what he done gave you. I heard these new strains of STDs can make you go blind if they go untreated. You ain't been itchin' or burnin' lately, have you?"

Mama Rose had a way of taking a bad situation and making it even more miserable, but in the end, I knew she would give me the perfect solution to fix Jayson for good.

"No, Mama Rose. I had a check-up last week and everything is fine."

"Well, that's good 'cause I'd hate to have to chop off his nuts and serve them to him for dinner for giving my baby the clap," she said, slicing a generous piece of carrot cake for me.

"God forbid he had given me something, but I still don't think chopping his stuff off is the answer," I said dropping a cube of sugar into the steaming hot tea cup.

I wondered where Mama Rose found sugar shaped in cubes during this day and age. Knowing Mama Rose, she probably ordered them from some expensive overseas store just to avoid the possible spill of sugar crystals on her spotless clean granite counters.

"Well, I don't know why not!" she exclaimed. "I had to straighten out your daddy a time or two. He was as stubborn as a mule and horny as a jack rabbit. He had so many women on the side, you would have thought that nappy-headed nigga was the King of Egypt."

"But you never cut daddy's stuff off, did you?" I asked hesitantly, my eyebrow arched. There was no telling what Mama Rose was capable of doing.

"Girl, naw! Of course I ain't cut that man's shit off, although I had good reason to. Plus, he ain't never brought no other child into this world by another woman, not that I know of. He learned his own lesson, anyway. See, when your daddy fell sick, none of them hussies he was cheating on me with took care of him or even bothered to find out if he was dead or alive. It was me and your sister who nursed and watched over him. To tell you the truth, I don't even think he appreciated it. I reckon he had a lot of explaining to do when he made it to the pearly gates - *if* that's where he ended up."

Whenever Mama Rose talked bad about my father, I wanted to plug my ears and hum a tune to block out all her salty words. I wanted to remember my father as the handsome, fun-loving, strong man that I always knew him to be. Not the ugly selfish man-whore she made him out as.

"The worst part is that I think he's been seeing this lady for over a year," I said, switching the subject from my father back to Jayson.

"Gen, I don't even know why you actin' all shocked and surprised about this whole thing. I done taught you and your sister from a very young age that a man will be a man. To expect anything else is your own idiotic indulgence. It's up to us as a woman to train these men. If a dog pisses on the carpet instead of on the newspaper like he's supposed to, you slap his dumb ass across the nose with the leash. Right? Why? Because every animal, even the dumb ones, understand pain."

"So what do you suggest I do, beat up my 6'2, 190 pound husband with my bare hands or slap him across the nose with a leash or newspaper?" I asked, sarcastically.

"No, just give him a little bit of this."

Mama Rose went into the cupboard a pulled out a small, brown leather pouch with a drawstring and placed it in my hand. The weathered skin of the bag indicated it had been around for many years, maybe even given to Mama Rose from her own mother.

"What's this?" I asked, curiously flipping the bag around looking for a label or some other indication of what was hidden inside this mysterious pouch.

I pulled it open and looked at the contents. What looked like tiny pieces of dried leaves and crumbled herbs covered the bottom of the soft leather pouch. The odorless earth tone pieces were so finely ground that it almost took on a powder form. I stuck the tip of my finger inside and brought it toward my lips.

"I wouldn't do that if I were you," Mama Rose cautioned, pulling my hand away from my face. Her grip was firm and her tone was stern.

"You act like its poison," I laughed, closing the bag and placing it down on the counter. Mama Rose looked at me with a blank expression. She didn't utter a word, but she didn't have to.

"You can't possibly think I want to kill Jayson!" I yelled.

I was appalled that my mother would suggest such a thing and shocked that she actually had a murder weapon hidden in her cupboard between her chamomile and peppermint tea and her bible.

"Calm down. No one said anything about killing anybody. Just put a couple of pinches of this in his tea or coffee every morning. Make sure to add a couple of teaspoons of sugar to cover up the bitterness. All that will happen is he'll start to feel a little under the weather after a week or so. His stomach will cramp, he'll have the shits like nobody's business and the headache of a lifetime, but it'll all pass. Ain't nothing wrong with giving a dog a taste of his own medicine. The hurt he done caused you ain't nothing compared to no migraine and the bubble guts. I say it serves him right."

Mama Rose casually flipped through the pages of an Essence magazine and took a sip of tea from her china cup like she hadn't just told me to do something that could get me manslaughter and 20 years to life in prison.

"I think I'd better get back home," I announced, getting up from the kitchen table and grabbing my purse.

"Don't forget the pouch," Mama Rose said, not bothering to look up from her magazine.

"I'm not going to use it."

I wiped my place setting with a napkin and made sure I left my area spotless like I knew she expected me to. Maybe coming to Mama Rose for advice had not been such a good idea.

"I've been praying for God to help me deal with this situation and I know this isn't the answer. I have faith God will lead me," I declared.

"If you do need it, then you'll have it on you and if you don't need it, well then, that's fine. But, it's always better to have than to have not," Mama Rose chirped.

I took the small bag and placed it deep at the bottom of my purse, just to appease Mama Rose. I didn't want her thinking I wasn't going to punish Jayson for his actions. So, I would pretend I gave it to him

and make up a story, someday next week, about him being on the toilet all day. She'd be satisfied and leave well enough alone. How could
I poison Jayson and condemn him for the same thing that I had been
doing? It hurt me that he had been with whoever *she* was for a year
when I had only been seeing Bret for a couple of months now, but I
guess two wrongs don't make a right.

"Thanks, Mama Rose," I mumbled, as I grabbed my car keys and
turned to let myself out.

"Mm hmm, don't forget: God helps those that help themselves,"
she replied.

Chapter 23

I was starting to wonder if someone somewhere had put some evil curse on me. It seemed like things had been going pretty sour starting a few years back. My unlucky streak all began with my affair with Professor Donovan and shit rolled downhill from there. First, there was the "accident", then I went to jail and Troy started whipping on Myeisha until she had a miscarriage. God knows, if I had been a free woman, I would have put two bullets in his skull and called it a day. When I met Jayson, I thought things were getting better, but come to find out, my partner till death do us part was seeing some off-brand bitch and now, Bret was threatening to tell Jayson about our affair. Bret was pressuring me to spend more and more time with him every day. If I refused, he would punish me by stopping by the house unexpectedly or ringing my cell phone off the hook. So far, Jayson did not suspect anything yet, but if Bret kept it up, it wouldn't be long before he did. But hell, things really couldn't get much worse. Or could they?

On one hand, I wanted to see Jayson's face when he found out I had been fucking his best friend behind his back. Not only would he see that two could play the game, but he would realize that I was better at it than he was. On the other hand, I knew I had to keep my affair with Bret hidden until the ball was in my park.

If someone had put a curse on me, I knew Madeline would know what to do, which was why I was driving down the Las Vegas strip on the way to her shop. Lifting my foot off of the gas pedal, I rolled alongside the curb. I didn't have to pull all the way up in the parking lot or get out of the car to see that the storefront had been vacated. The fluorescent open sign and purple drapes that had once hung in the window were now gone. My heart sank. I was hoping she could give me some protection - a talisman, a magic potion or maybe she knew some type of reverse spell to get rid of my dark cloud. I had come prepared with $50,000 that I had taken from me and Jayson's joint account this morning. It was a large sum of money, but a small price to pay for my future and happiness. Besides, it was $50,000 less that Jayson could spend flaunting his whore around town. I wondered why Madeline had packed up and left. Maybe she was a fraud after all. Some crazy-ass, backwards bitch from the sticks who was pretending to be blind while preying on the vulnerability of naïve superstitious, rich city folk and I was one of the ones who let her get in my head. I guess that made me dumb and Madeline the smartest blind person I had ever had the opportunity of meeting. I peeled out leaving a dust cloud and my trepidations over evil curses and hexes behind.

Despite my recent discovery of Jayson's affair, I felt in good spirits. I had even gotten up early this morning to share a cup of coffee with him before he headed off to work or wherever he was actually going. For all I knew, he was getting all fancied up to go see his mistress and only pretending to be going into the office.

"You're up mighty early today," Jayson had commented as he stirred creamer into his cup of joe.

"Yeah, I have some business to take care of today, so I have to get up and moving," I stated chirpily.

"Oh, are you volunteering at the shelter today?"

"Uh... yeah. They're real busy, so they were happy to hear from me," I lied straight-faced.

Since I didn't know the truth about Jayson's daily whereabouts or anything else for that matter, I figured I had no obligation to be truthful to him.

"I might not be home until after dinner time," I added, deciding I would probably schedule a session with Bret this evening. I needed some release and even though I was determined to live under the same roof and remain civil with Jayson until I could think of the perfect plan to get him back, there was no way I would be having sex with him.

"I think it's great that you found something to keep you busy. Have a good day and don't worry about being home for dinner. I doubt I'll be able to break away from the office until around eight or nine tonight." He kissed me on the check, grabbed his keys and left.

As soon as the door slammed, I took a napkin and scrubbed the remnants of his soiled lips off my cheek. I wanted to scream after him, 'You have a good day, too! Don't forget to clean your tramp's filthy juices off your dirty dick before you come home! Oh and, by the way, I'm fucking your best friend tonight, so don't rush home for dinner!'

Our relationship was too broken to be fixed. My emotions were a whirlpool of mixed sentiments. Although I yearned for Jayson and what could have been, I hated what he had done. I hated myself for believing that he would be any different than Professor Donovan or any other man in my life, including my father. All the men that lied, saying they loved me and would always be there for me. Maybe Mama Rose was right. Men are not capable of love, honesty or commitment. And I didn't want or need any of them any longer. They were incapable of satisfying me. All I wanted was revenge and if it was as sweet as I dreamed it to be, only then could I be satisfied.

Chapter 24

My blood was boiling and my heart was pounding. I wished I had the double-barrel shotgun my great-grandmother had left my mother when she passed. It was the only firearm anyone I knew owned. My great-grandmother had been a feistier version of Mama Rose. The single mother of three daughters, including my mother, and two sons, she learned to be the provider, the protector and the backbone of her family. Growing up in her era in the south wasn't easy. With four kids and a farm to protect, she believed in the policy, Shoot first and ask questions later. Many a person had stared down its long stock. I'm sure the majority of them had rethought whatever action they had done to wind them up in that situation and backed down. Others, I'm sure, either drunk or just plain stupid, had tested Great-Grandma Lily and taken her warning as an empty threat from some old, incompetent, senile hag. Those souls ended up regretting their choice from the other side of the pearly gates.

"I'm coming over there right now! If that sorry sack of shit lays one more hand on you, I'm going to get a gun and blow his head off. If he's standing there threatening you or listening to you, tell him exactly what I just said!"

I was infuriated and screaming at the top of my lungs. It obviously hadn't taken long for Troy to forget his training from all the anger management classes he had taken while in jail. It had only been two weeks since his release and he was already whipping on Myeisha like she was his personal punching bag. She had just called and told me that he had punched her in the face and given her a black eye just because she cooked spaghetti with no meatballs.

Bitch, how the fuck you gonna cook dinner with no damn meat on the plate? Hell, when I was locked down, I ate better than this shit, she said he had spat at her before tossing the plate in the garbage and slamming his closed fist into her face.

"D-don't come here, Gen," Myeisha stammered nervously.

"Why? Is that motherfucker still there? Forget it, I'm calling 911."

"No!" Myeisha yelled. Her feeble voice went up two octaves. "If you call the police, it'll just make trouble for me. Besides, he left in my car right after he hit me. Plus, he'll tell about the bank," Myeisha stated, hesitantly, her voice back down to a mere whisper.

"He'll tell what about the bank?"

"Well, Troy met this guy in jail named Lucius. They got released around the same time. Troy owed Lucius a favor, so he asked me to cash a couple of checks for Lucius that were fake. He said I only had to do it a couple of times, but a couple of times turned into more like five or six."

"I'm surprised the bank hasn't already caught on yet, Myeisha. You could lose your job over this and even worse, you could go to jail."

"The bank hasn't caught on because Lucius sends different people to cash the checks. Candance is in on it, too, so sometimes, I send them to her window. That way, it just doesn't seem like I'm the only teller getting bad checks. They'll think it's just some crooks coming in and trying to get over."

"No, they won't! They'll think you and Candance, the only two black tellers, are doing some underhanded shit. And, they'll be right. Myeisha, promise me you won't do it again and I promise you I won't call the police."

"I promise," Myeisha said. She sounded drained and defeated.

"Okay. I won't call the police, but I'm coming over."

Before I could get a response, I was out of bed and throwing on my pink velour sweat suit and a pair of Nikes. I glanced at the clock. It was 2 in the morning and Jayson was still not at home. I clenched my jaw in frustration. Even after seeing Bret this evening, I was able to make it home at 8 pm. Jayson was being audacious with his extra-curricular activities. Maybe he had noticed my recent callousness and disregard toward him lately. I never cooked dinner anymore. What was the point? He was never at home to eat it. I diverted any sexual advances he made by telling him I was one my period (for two weeks straight now). I had even stopped washing his laundry. I'm sure his whore wouldn't mind washing his dirty underwear. Maybe he understood that I was trying to distance myself from him and he was taking advantage of the opportunity to do the same. I didn't have time to try to figure out why Jayson wasn't at home or why he hadn't at least called to check in. Since it was Friday night, he would probably make up some lie about hanging out with his colleagues at Posh. Right now, I had to be there for my friend. I hadn't been able to be there for her before, but this time, I was not going to let her down. There was no way I was going to stand by and allow Troy's ignorant, convict-ass to hurt my best friend again. There was going to be hell to pay for him putting his mangy hands on Myeisha. There was going to be hell to pay for any man that thought he was going to use or abuse me or any woman close to me. I was tired of men and their lies, the hurt they caused and the pain they dealt out like blackjack dealers. Like Mama Rose always told me when I was a child, right before I got a lashing with a switch for getting in trouble, bad grades or talking back: 'There's a consequence for every action in due time. But if due time don't come fast enough, I'm gone be the one to bring it swiftly.'

Chapter 25

I pushed the alarm button on my key ring to make sure the doors to my Jaguar were locked. I hated parking my car in Myeisha's seedy neighborhood. The last time I came over, some bum had run a shopping cart into my bumper by mistake. Luckily, it hadn't made a dent or scratched the paint. Another time, I had caught some thugs checking out my rims like they were up for grabs. The experiences made me weary to leave my car unattended.

I could hear Myeisha fumbling with the locks on the other side of her apartment door. When she finally got it open, I had to conceal my shock and control the gasp that threatened to escape my lips. Her petite elf-like features were distorted and enlarged. The bruising around her left eye had swollen shut and spread to her cheek. She looked like a chipmunk with a stash of nuts in its mouth.

"I think you need to see a doctor, Myeisha," I said, trying not to sound too alarmed.

"I know, it looks pretty bad, but it's mostly swelling. It'll go down in a day a two if I keep ice on it. As luck has it, I'm off for the entire weekend," she spoke nonchalantly, as she placed a sandwich bag full of ice to the side of her eye. I felt sorry for her. She knew exactly how long it would take for her eye to heal and how to nurse her wounds because it wasn't the first time Troy had given her a black eye. Before he got locked up, he was beating on her for breakfast, lunch and dinner.

She plopped down on the couch. I sat next to her and placed my hand on her lap. We sat silently for a while. I didn't know what she was thinking, but I was hoping she was thinking that things had to change, that Troy hitting her was as old and played out as the electric slide.

"You were right," she said, breaking the silence. "Troy and I aren't going to work out, but I've already let him move in and he's not going to leave me alone that easily. I know I need to leave him alone, but he's already told me that if I thought things were bad now, just wait and see what will happen if I try to leave."

"Change the locks, get a retaining order, move in with Jayson and I. Whatever you do you have to make the steps to leave him and I promise I will help you."

"Gen, I tried all of those things the last time. A restraining order is a useless piece of paper the court invented to try to act like they're doing something for domestic violence victims that come to them for help, so when they end up dead, they can say, 'We tried to help'. I changed the locks and he kicked the door down. Moving in with you will only bring you more trouble than you already have. Besides, it won't stop him. Like I said on the phone, if I call the police, he'll tip the bank off about what I've been doing. Gen, I don't know what to do!"

Myeisha burst into tears, allowing all of her bottled up agony to be released.

"I do," I murmured.

The idea had come to me suddenly and clearly. I remembered how I was willing to do anything to escape my flood of bad luck that I had believed had been prophesized by Madeline. I wondered if Troy believed Myeisha was his source of bad luck, would it make him leave willingly.

Put a couple of pinches of this in his tea or coffee every morning. Ain't nothing wrong with giving a dog a taste of his own medicine.

I could hear Mama Rose's southern drawl just as clearly as if she were sitting next to me instead of Myeisha.

I dug deep into the bottom of my purse and pulled out the worn leather bag that Mama Rose had given me just the other day.

"Does Troy drink coffee or tea?" I asked, with a smile on my face.

Chapter 26

"How are things between you and Jayson?" Bret asked. We were lying together in his bed. The bedroom was filled with the sultry tune of Sade's voice. *Smooth operator... smooth operator.*

His arm was wrapped around my waist. I tousled his blonde strands with my fingertips.

"Why do you ask?"

"You're my girl just as much as you're his. I wanna make sure he's treating you right, too."

"Everything's fine."

Although I knew Jayson was creeping around, everything was still fine in my book. If he wanted to divorce me, I would take half. I had already started slowly moving small sums of money from our joint account to my own private account, which already held my one million, at a different bank that he knew nothing about. Once I finalized my plans to get back at him, things would be more than fine - they would be dandy.

"Are you sure?" Bret pressed on, as if he knew something that I didn't know.

I sat up and looked Bret in the eyes. From the way he had trouble keeping eye contact and was shifting jerkily from side to side, I knew he was hiding something.

"What is it Bret? You're his best friend. Maybe you know something I don't know, something you need to tell me right now before things get real ugly round here!"

"Okay, okay, calm down," Bret said, holding up both hands. He got out of the bed and wrapped the edge of the bed sheet around his waist. He took a few steps back, creating space between me and him.

"I didn't want to be the one to tell you this. I wanted Jayson to step up and be a man. I wanted him to tell you the truth. When he didn't, I tried to let you see for yourself. That's why I took you to the Japanese restaurant that day. I knew Jayson would be there with her."

"You what!?" I exclaimed.

He was right to distance himself from me. If he had still been next to me in the bed, I probably would have slapped the taste from his mouth.

"I wasn't trying to hurt you. I just thought it was your right to know that you're husband is an adulterer. Actually, he's a bigamist."

Bret took another step back. I jumped out of the bed and was in front of him in a flash, butt-naked and titties swinging. He had no time to retreat.

"You tell me what you're talking about right now!" I yelled pointing my finger in Bret's face.

"Jayson is married to another lady. He met her couple of years before he met you. She got pregnant and they eloped. Jayson kept her a secret from everyone. I'm the only one who knows the truth."

"They have a child?" I whispered.

"A girl. She should be a year this month."

To a year. They had been cheering to their daughter's first birthday the night I saw them at Geisha.

Large, warm drops of tears splattered onto my chest. Bret approached me cautiously and embraced me.

"I'm sorry, Gen. I didn't want to hurt you, but you have the right to know. He and the judge that granted your marriage license are golfing buddies, so it was easy for him to get away with the legalities of his behavior and morally, he could care less. He's an arrogant, selfish bastard who doesn't deserve a woman like you."

I felt battered and bruised like Myeisha, only just from the inside. My heart ached so bad, I thought I might be going into cardiac arrest.

"I saw him at Geisha. I had suspected that he was cheating long before that, but I never in my wildest dreams would think he was actually married to another woman or that he had a child with someone else. Why... why did he marry me *and* her?" I moaned.

"Because he can," Bret replied. "He's no good. You need to leave him, Gen."

"I will," I said, wiping snot and tears from my face with the back of my hand. But, first, I want you to tell me everything you know about her. Her name, where she lives, where she works, everything."

I was already starting to calm down. I had to be clear-headed if I wanted to devise a plan good enough to bring a man like Jayson to his knees.

"Gen, she doesn't know about you. It's not her fault. I think you should leave her out of it," Bret stated.

"Look, this is simple, Bret. If you don't tell me everything you know about her, including when she takes a shit and how hard it is, then it's over between us. You'll never see me again. You can't threaten me by saying you're going to tell Jayson about us anymore because I don't give a fuck what he thinks. He can go to hell and you can too if you don't tell me everything."

"Can I pour myself a scotch first? " Bret asked, defeated.

"Sure, pour me one too and make it a double because it's going to be a long night," I replied.

Chapter 27

J ayson was a busy man. Not only did he have two wives, a child and a career as a promising attorney, he also owned two beautiful homes within one block of each other. Being the multi-tasker that he was, he needed to house both of his women in close proximity of each other for convenience and accessibility. I assume if he could have it his way, he would have had us all live together as one, big, happy, polygamist family. He would sleep with me on Tuesdays, Thursdays and Saturdays and his other wife, Jasmine, would have all the other days in between. If he got lucky, we could even have threesomes from time to time. We would also take turns cooking, cleaning and taking care of him and his child. This, I'm sure, was his and countless other male chauvinist pigs' wildest fantasy. Each time Bret unveiled one of Jayson's dirty secrets, I couldn't help but be dumbfounded that I had been sleeping with a complete stranger all of this time.

Jasmine and his daughter, Jewel, were hidden treasures that even Jayson's own mother didn't know existed. When they met, she was an exotic dancer. He became infatuated with her, but the relationship was built only upon his sexual attraction to her. He would never think of letting his colleagues know that he had fallen for a stripper. He couldn't take her to his social functions, be seen with her in public or take her home to momma. She was a hood girl with a tainted history that, according to Bret, included ties with the pornography industry. Jayson wasn't counting on her getting pregnant. A child out of wedlock with a sex worker could ruin his reputation, so he married her to keep her quiet. I was his trophy wife - the one with etiquette from a well-off family, pursuing a degree in Psychology. Since Jayson had made sure I was acquitted on all charges, I was untarnished, unlike his first wife. He could take me to his mother's for Thanksgiving and Christmas and I could mingle with his boss and co-workers at Franklin and Franklin, but as much as it seemed like I was the privileged wife, I wasn't. Since he had married Jasmine first, it made my marriage to Jayson a fraud. If I was to leave him, I would get nothing. That essential detail made me reconsider my game plan.

***

"You really think highlights would look good on me?" Myeisha asked, running her fingers through her freshly cut, chic, short hair-do. Neeka held a small mirror in her hand and spun her around in the chair, so that she could see the back of her head. "Ooh, you hooked me up! The back looks even better than the front."

"When you come in next week, I can do a few light highlights here and there. If you like it, we'll make it more noticeable the next time," Neeka said, brushing pieces of hair from the back of Myeisha's neck and ears.

I was happy to see Myeisha back to her normal self again. Since Troy had come back in the picture, she hadn't been her usual sassy, up-beat, crazy self. Her usually incessant chatter had been reduced to a few occasional monotone blurbs that I had to drag out of her. Everywhere we went, she watched her back and scanned the room, as if Troy was hiding in a corner somewhere, watching her every move. Her once perfectly manicured nails were gnawed down to the skin and her bright glow was dimming. I was thankful that she had agreed to leave the house and take a trip to Oh So Natural. Neeka had worked her magic, as usual, and had my girl smiling from ear to ear.

"Let's go to the mall and pick up some new outfits to go with your new look. I'm buying," I said to Myeisha, handing Neeka my charge card.

"I can't... it's getting late," Myeisha said, looking at the silver watch on her wrist.

"What are you talking about? It's only 4 o'clock. I know you aren't trying to rush home on account of that punk-ass bitch you call a man."

I made sure to keep my voice low. Although Neeka had walked up front to swipe my card at the register, there was an endless amount of nosy hairdressers and gossipy clients milling about that I didn't want to overhear our conversation.

"He didn't go into work today. He said he was feeling a bit under the weather. You know, stomach issues and stuff like that."

Myeisha tossed me a 'if you know what I mean' look, then glanced back down at her watch.

"I have to go home and fix him some soup for dinner or he'll throw a fit." Me and her both knew what she really meant was, "or he'll beat the holy shit out of me."

I couldn't understand how she tolerated Troy. Even though he had some job washing dishes at a restaurant, he wouldn't give Myeisha a dime of his money to help with the bills around the house. He ate her food, drove her car, slept in her bed and had the nerve to tell her that he was not going to help with the bills until she learned to "act right". I had told Myeisha that I could get Jayson or Bret to pull a few strings and have him thrown in jail, without involving her. She refused, stating he would only get out and cause more trouble if he thought she had anything to do with it. She didn't have the nerve to stand up to him legally, but at least she was following some of my advice. She had been slipping some of the contents from the small brown bag I had given her into Troy's coffee thermos every morning before he went to work. On the first day, Myeisha said he complained of a bloated stomach. On the second day, he stayed on the toilet a lot. Now, on the third day, he was calling out of work, sick. He probably had the runs so bad, he had a ring around his butt from sitting on the toilet so much. I found humor in his agony and thought about asking Myeisha to give the pouch back to me after she was done so I could try it on Jayson, after all.

"Okay, maybe we can go shopping another day," I agreed, fishing in my purse for my keys.

Neeka handed me my card back and me and Myeisha thanked her and headed towards the exit.

"Mmm, mmm, mmm," Jordan, the ignorant beautician that both Myeisha and I loved to hate, grunted as we walked past her station. She had changed her hair from bright red to a hideous orange-copper color. That and the dreadful blue eye-shadow and pink lipstick she had on made her look like a circus clown. We kept walking and ignored her remark. As much as I wanted to check her, I didn't want Myeisha to be exposed to anymore drama than what was already going on at her home.

"These bitches think they the shit," Jordan announced to her client who sat squinting in fear, as Jordan pulled a sizzling hot pressing comb through her hair.

Myeisha's attention stayed focused on the exit. I could tell she was more concerned with getting home to Troy than she was with Jordan's nasty comment. The bitch remark did it for me, though, and unfortunately for Jordan, she had pushed the button of a woman who was already on the edge. I stopped dead in my tracks and did an about-face. Jordan stopped pressing her client's hair and stared at me. Her expression said 'you ain't going to do nothing,' but her body was poised in anticipation of an attack.

"Let me tell you something, you no-class, back-stabbing, sloppy bitch. We don't think we the shit - we know we the shit. If we weren't, then lonely, trifling bitches like you wouldn't sit around and talk about us all day."

Jordan came from behind her client's stool and took two gigantic thunderous steps toward me. Her massive frame towered over my small frame. She grasped the pressing comb in her hand like a weapon. My eyes skimmed the closet station's counter. I grabbed a pair of shiny cutting scissors from a nearby cart.

"If you even think of burning me with that comb, I'll cut you so fast, you won't even know it happened," I threatened her.

I couldn't believe I was in public, ready to fight like a high-schooler. I didn't come here to pick a fight. Anyone could see that. I was wearing a tailored plaid pencil skirt, a black silk blouse and stilettos - a far cry from fighting gear. However, I wasn't in the mood to put up with Jordan's bullshit. Everyone crowded around us. I could hear

Neeka from somewhere in the crowd, saying, "Come on, ladies, everyone calm down." But I was more distracted by Myeisha pulling on my arm. "Gen, we gotta go right now!"

"Myeisha, let go of me. If this bitch want some, then I'll give it to her," I said all too calmly as I yanked my arm away from Myeisha.

Myeisha grabbed my arm again, squeezing so firmly, she nearly cut off my circulation.

"I said let go!" I yelled at Myeisha and turned to face her. A look of pure terror and alarm was on her face. She held her cell phone up to her right ear while she pulled me forcefully with her left arm.

"It's the hospital on the phone! Troy's been admitted to the hospital. They don't know if he's going to make it. We need to get there right now!" Myeisha screamed.

I dropped the scissors. They clattered to the floor. Jordan smirked and put down the hot comb. I allowed Myeisha to guide me out the door and into the car. I was still registering what had just happened in the shop and what Myeisha had just told me. We drove to the hospital in a panic.

"Do you think it was the stuff in the bag? What do I say if they ask me about anything he's eaten or drank in the last few days?" Myeisha asked worriedly as we pulled in to the parking lot.

She was only saying what we had both been thinking the whole drive to the hospital. What if we had killed Troy?

"You don't say anything. Let me do the talking," I told her.

Myeisha was crying when we walked through the hospital doors and into the lobby. I didn't know if she was in tears over Troy's welfare or over the heap of shit that was about to hit the fan.

Chapter 28

Myeisha took two apprehensive shuffles towards the hospital bed like she was approaching a ticking bomb or kryptonite. She looked over Troy's still body. He looked a lot like Professor Donovan had the last time I saw him - in an infinite sleep, tubes protruding from everywhere. She looked over her shoulder pitifully at me and the doctor.

"At least he seems pretty stable now. For a while, it was touch and go there, but he's a pretty tough guy and he wasn't going to give up that easily," the tall, slender, corky, young doctor stated.

He seemed more energetic and free-spirited than most of the stuffy old doctors I had encountered. He was also quite handsome and personable. If I would have seen Dr. Monroe on the street without his name tag or white physician's coat, I would have mistaken him as the model or actor sort.

Yeah, all cockroaches are hard to kill, I thought to myself about Troy.

"It would really help us out a lot if you could write down a list of everything he has eaten within the last 48 hours. Also, if he's eaten at any restaurants within that timeframe, you can jot down their name and specific location, too," Dr. Monroe said, handing Myeisha a small square tablet and a pen.

"Okay, sure," she said, taking the pen and pad from Dr. Monroe. Her hand shook so violently, I was afraid she would drop them both on the floor, but Dr. Monroe squeezed her hands, gently steading them.

"Don't worry, your boyfriend's not out of the woodwork yet, but he's in good hands," he advised. "We are running extensive lab tests on him and it would benefit him greatly if you could help us to isolate the source of his illness. It definitely seems to be some type of food poisoning, however, his is much more acute than most cases that I have seen. A detailed list of the foods he has eaten and restaurants he has visited in the last couple of days would be helpful."

Myeisha froze, staring at the doctor with a look of guilt so apparent that Dr. Monroe wrinkled his nose in confusion.

"Uh hmm, I said, clearing my throat and the thick air. I was watching the whole scene unfold from the hospital room doorway. "This is really devastating to her; they were going to be engaged. She's probably in shock. I'm her best friend, Genevieve. I'll help her put the list together."

I extended my hand to the doctor. He held my hand for longer than normal. There was a connection, an attraction between us.

"You're a good friend for helping her through this," Dr. Monroe said, our eyes were locked together.

"Thanks, Dr. Monroe," I blushed.

"Call me Daniel," he said, as he slowly brushed past me and left the room.

"Come on, Myeisha, you have got to pull yourself together," I said, wrapping my arm around her fragile shoulders. She was still standing over Troy's bed. Her body was trembling with heart-wrenching sobs. It was obvious that she was not good at lying or controlling her conscience. She had been like that since I could remember. One time in high school, she got us both put on punishment for the entire summer when she confessed to her mother that we had ditched the last day of school. I was surprised she had been able to keep up her scheme at the bank without telling on herself in one way or another. I hoped the police wouldn't get involved and have to ask her any questions. It would be hard for her not to crack under pressure, but there was no way I was going to let anyone lock her away like some heinous villain over the sack of shit lying in the bed in front of us.

"M-maybe we should tell them what we gave him. We don't have to let them know *we* gave it to him. If it will help them treat him, we could just tell them…"

I closed the door to the room, thankful Troy wasn't sharing a room with any other patients and I interrupted Myeisha before she could finish her last poorly thought out sentence.

"And tell them what Myeisha? That Troy always sprinkles arsenic or whatever was in that bag on his food at breakfast? Be real, of course they will know you had something to do with it!"

"Arsenic!?" Myeisha exclaimed.

"Sshhh! Lower your freakin' voice before you get us both put in jail," I said, placing my hand over her mouth.

She pulled my hand away, but kept her voice down to a whisper.

"But I thought you said it was a laxative of something. Remember, you said it would just make him go to the bathroom like crazy."

"Look, Mama Rose gave me the bag. I don't think its arsenic or poison, but honestly, I really don't know what was in that bag."

"Well, you need to find out. I don't want him to die and I definitely don't want to be serving time in prison for first-degree murder."

"Okay, I'll talk to Mama Rose and find out what was in the bag, but you have got to lay low until then. Go home and get some rest. If anybody calls - the cops, the hospital or anybody at all - just let the answering machine pick up. Do not open your door and do not talk to anyone!"

Myeisha nodded in agreement.

I had wanted to punish Troy, but I didn't count on things turning out the way they had. Myeisha was right. If we could give Dr. Monroe the information he needed to help Troy, then maybe we could still save his life... and our butts.

Chapter 29

Mama Rose never had much pity for men. She felt that any pain or suffering they experienced had been well-earned by them in some way. Even when my father took ill and passed away, she had no pity for him in his last moments.

"Elroy Lee Johnson." She always called him by his whole name whenever she was chastising him. "I thank you for giving me my wonderful daughters and I wish we could have made things right between us at least for them, but the truth is you wouldn't have stopped cheating on me, even if God gave you a chance to have your life back. When you leave this earth, I want you to remember who was there for you at the end. Not any of those hussies you was creeping around with at the juke joint. No, it was your wife and your daughters. Now, you take that thought to your grave."

That was the goodbye speech my mother had given my father as she sat on the edge of the wooden bed they had consummated their marriage on and bore two children in. She served him, what would be his last cup of tea and tomato soup, before leaving the room, with me and my sister at the foot of his bed, wondering why she would say such nasty things to our father when he was obviously so fragile.

She had not changed much over the years. She had dated here and there since my father, but she never again committed to another man. I dreamed it was because she was so in love with my father that no one else could ever take his place, but I knew it was really because she despised men and would never let another one get close enough to her to cause the same pain she had experienced before.

"White Oleander. That's what was in the pouch, along with a touch of Jimson weed," Mama Rose said, taking a swig of brandy from a sparkling crystal glass. We were sitting in her living room on her tan, suede chaise that she usually never allowed anyone to lay a finger, much less, lounge on it.

"White Oleander… I've heard of that, it's a flower, right?" I asked, longingly following the glass up to Mama Rose's red painted lips. She had offered me a drink and I had desperately wanted to accept it, but I figured I needed to stay clear-minded, in order to straighten out this mess. She held the cup with her pinkie finger in the air. Mama Rose was a charming southern belle at first glance, but a closer look could reveal the vicious piranha she really was.

"Well, of course it is. It's an extremely dangerous one, if digested. But, really, it's just a flower," she replied, as if we were having a conversation about leisurely gardening instead on someone's life.

"Well, obviously he digested it or he wouldn't be in the hospital and we wouldn't be having this conversation."

"I really don't know why you and Myeisha are getting so upset over all of this. He's not going to die. The amount I gave you in the pouch wasn't enough to kill a bird, much less, a grown-ass man.

You're both overreacting and if you tell them folks at the hospital anything of the sort, you just going to cause a heap of problems for yourselves."

Mama Rose stood up and walked to the window staring out. It was her way of telling me that she wanted the conversation to end there, but I wasn't finished yet.

"Troy is in the hospital fighting for his life. Myeisha called me just before I came over and said that one of his kidneys failed and he might need dialysis and you think we are overreacting?"

"I said it once and I'll say it again: You are both overreacting. Troy put his hands on Myeisha one too many times and she apparently got fed up and decided to fight back. Now, she's having regrets because she's a weak woman. Myeisha is one thing, but you are another, Genevieve. I didn't raise you to be weak and take pity on those that wouldn't take pity on you."

Mama Rose turned around, glaring at me with fire in her eyes.

"Now, you listen and you listen good," she said. "You came to me for help, as any daughter should come to her mother for guidance and direction when she's in need. I gave you sound advice: to give Jayson a taste of his own medicine. Not only did you disregard my advice, but you continued to allow Jayson to run around the city, spreading his seed like it's his profession. Then, you involved yourself in your friend's affairs when you haven't even taken care of your own business at home. If I didn't know any better, I'd think a pack of retarded raccoons raised you 'cause you actin' like you ain't got a lick of sense, child! You got something much more dangerous brewing at home: a man with another woman and another child who happens to hold the state of your future in his hands. I know you are smarter than what you been puttin' on lately. If Jayson found a way to get married twice and not get caught, then you can surely find a way to make sure that you're the wife that walks away from this with the most dignity. Now, stop pestering me and find a way to get that man of yours back in check before he leaves you looking like the World's Biggest Fool."

Mama Rose was right. I had been investing so much time and energy into Myeisha and her situation that I had forgotten to deal with my own. Troy would be okay, and if he wasn't, well, it served him right. Regardless of the fact that I was Jayson's second wife, I had to make it very clear to him I was the only wife that mattered. If he wanted his career and finances to remain intact, then he would see things just as clearly as I did and things would work out just fine.

Chapter 30

"Good morning, beautiful!" Jayson said, while stretching and yawning, his mouth stretched open as wide as a hungry lion.

"Morning," I mumbled, covering my nose with a cupped hand. His jolliness was annoying and his breath was atrocious. He got out of bed and turned on the clock radio. Funkadelic music from the 70s blasted from its speakers.

"Play that funky music white boy!" Jayson sang at the top of his lungs. I didn't know what had gotten into him, but he was in an unusually upbeat mood. Last night, he and Bret had hung out at Posh together. When he told me he was going to meet with Bret, I was happy that they were getting along and communicating again. This meant that Bret had not spilled the beans and Jayson didn't suspect anything. On the flip-side, I was apprehensive about what could happen if they started drinking and sharing laughs. Would Bret slip up and mistakenly give clues of our infidelity? Would he suddenly remember that his loyalty lay with his best friend since high school and confess to

Jayson that he has been sleeping with his wife for the past three months at least three times a week?

Jayson ignored my rude gesture and danced around the room like he was in the Soul Train line.

"You're in a good mood this morning. You and Bret must've had a nice time last night," I said, fishing for information.

"Yeah, we did. Bret seemed like his old self again. I guess he had some things on his mind, but whatever it was, he seems like he's moved on now."

Jayson walked to the bathroom and squirted a lump of white paste onto his toothbrush. My nostrils would thank him for it. I watched him methodically scrub his teeth up and down and side to side in the same pattern over and over before I finally slid on my slippers and shuffled into the bathroom next to him. I brushed my teeth quietly while Jayson hummed to the music. I couldn't imagine thirty more years next to this man. As a matter of fact, thirty more seconds were straining enough.

"You know what?" I started, slamming my toothbrush down in the sink.

I knew I was breaking. I felt incapable of holding back my true feelings with Jayson any longer. There was nothing particular about the situation that made me want to let him know that I knew he was a low-life, cheating pig, but I itched with the notion to tell him everything, including the part that I was sleeping with Bret to pay him back.

"I have a headache, so I would appreciate it if you can keep all the racket down to a minimum," I said, barely able to maintain my composure.

"Well... okay," he said, studying my reflection in the mirror. "Is there anything I can do to make you feel better?"

Sure there is... drop dead and leave all your money to me, asshole, I thought to myself.

Mama Rose was right. I needed to pay more attention to my own affairs at home. Jayson and Bret had both become baggage that I could live without. However, I needed to unpack all of my necessities before tossing out the luggage. I needed to make sure Jayson would not be able to walk away from our marriage and leave me penniless and destitute. Bret was my ticket to make sure that didn't occur. He had all the contacts throughout the court system, including judges and other authorities, to make sure I walked away a winner.

"Not really, but thanks for asking," I said, wishing I hadn't almost lost my temper and spilled the beans.

"I think I have the perfect remedy."

Jayson grabbed my hand and placed it on the hardness that had grown in his pants. I jerked my hand away like his penis was engulfed in red hot flames. Jayson frowned, letting me know that I had upset him. His soft, brown eyes and pleading, puppy dog face would have worked any other time. It would have easily swayed me if I didn't know that he was had a whole other family stashed away just a block over.

"It's been a long time since we've been intimate, Gen. Is something wrong?" He brushed a loose strand from my cheek and placed his hand on the side of my face.

For a brief moment, I wanted to give in to his magnetism, but he had made it impossible for me to do so. There was no way I could ever forget that Jasmine and Jewel existed. They were my reality just as much as they were his.

"I know our paths have not crossed much lately. You have been really busy at work and I have been putting in a lot of hours at the shelter. I promise I'll make it up to you when things slow down."

It was easy to put some of the blame back on him. He was never at home, always using the excuse that he was working on a case, but we both knew the truth.

"Well, I hope that's soon because I won my case yesterday in court. Mr. Westings was exonerated. His wife and her lover's plot to have him killed was uncovered and the court acknowledged his actions as self-defense," Jayson said, smiling proudly from ear to ear.

"Congratulations, I bet you're a hero in Mr. Westings' eyes and at the firm."

"It was a very high profile case and I received a lot of recognition from it. Just yesterday, I've had two messages on my cell phone, offering me positions at other firms. And the incentives in their offers are really making me consider their propositions. My loyalty lies with Franklin and Franklin since they hired me fresh out of law school and gave me the opportunity to learn and grow, but I have to move on sooner or later."

I knew leaving Franklin and Franklin would be a hard thing for him to do, but he was right. He needed to expand, explore different options and take new paths in his career.

"So, have you decided what you're going to do?" I asked.

"It wasn't an easy decision, but after talking to Bret last night, I decided to stick to my original plan and open up a firm with him."

I tried to hide my alarm at his statement by concentrating on a pimple on my chin in the mirror. Something was obviously wrong with this picture. Bret had clearly expressed to me that he no longer had any desire to open a firm with Jayson. Plain and simple, Bret despised Jayson, which made the fact that he met with him last night and discussed business plans like they were best buddies again, quite strange.

"Well...?" Jayson asked, urging me for a response.

"Well, what? Why are you asking me for my opinion? It's your career, not mine," I stated, matter of factly.

"Because you're my wife," he responded gently.

"Oh really!? That's funny because I didn't think that title carried much weight with you," I said before walking out of the bathroom and leaving Jayson wondering how much wifey number two really knew.

Chapter 31

If life throws you a curve ball, I say throw one back. I hadn't counted on Jayson being married and having a child and I really hadn't counted on coming in second place. Here I was, worrying about Jayson cheating on me, when all along, he was cheating *with* me. It's kind of funny how the only thing you can always count on is things not working out like you expected. That's why I was glad Momma Rose had taught me to always be prepared.

"A real woman is ready for war, even on the best of days. That's why I always carry a tube of lip stick, a pack of crackers and my .45 wherever I go," Momma Rose had said, tapping her black leather handbag as me, her and Georgette walked to church for Saturday night bible study. Although many years had passed since she made that statement, I would never forget how right she was.

A week later, I went on my very first date with Ronnie Parker - a shy, scrawny kid with no backbone, but a heart the size of Texas. The only reason Momma Rose even let me go out with him was because he attended the same church as us and she knew he was too ugly for any girl in their right mind to allow him to lay a finger on them. When a group of thugs from a rival school tried to jump him on the way to dinner, I scared them away by telling them I carried a gun in my purse, although the closest thing I had to a weapon in my bag was tweezers. They got away with his wallet, which contained our money for dinner and a taxi home. But thanks to Momma Rose's advice, we didn't go hungry and I still looked cute after our 5 mile walk back home.

Jayson may have thought he caught me slippin', but a woman like me was always up on her game. Bret was more useful out of the bedroom than he was in. His connections in court were proving to be more valuable than his bedside manners. He had already had a friend with the county records department switch the dates in the database to show me as the first wife and Jasmine as the second wife. That way when I filed for divorce, Jayson would be financially obligated to me. Bret had also contacted the judge who had married Jayson and Jasmine. If any question regarding their marriage were to arise, Bret made sure the judge would confirm their marriage as being a complete sham. The dirt Bret had collected on the judge's personal sex life was enough for him to go with our story. If they tried to produce the original marriage certificate, I'd just argue that it was a fake. I would have county records and my own revised marriage certificate to support my argument. Case closed.

I wondered how long it would take for Jayson to realize that I had changed our marriage records and was slowly emptying his bank account, day by day. My actions might be frowned upon as uncalled for; some might even classify me as an evil, vindictive bitch, but I say, "All is fair in love and war."

"You have to come to the hospital," Myeisha breathed into the phone. Her voice vibrated with panic. I rolled over in bed and whispered into the phone. Bret was lying next to me. The smile on his face let me know he was dreaming sweet dreams.

"I'm busy right now, Myeisha."

Frankly, I was tired of Myeisha's pouting and whining over Troy. He had been in the hospital for almost two weeks now, but he was doing much better and they were supposed to let him go within the next couple of days. His kidneys had been pushed to the maximum of their ability, so he would be required to return to the hospital for dialysis treatments for a while until they were fully able to function on their own again, but even with that minor detail, I would say everything worked out great. The hundreds of lab tests the hospital staff ran did not reveal the source of his illness. No one suspected any foul play. Myeisha's guilty conscience was the only thing keeping us hostage to the situation. She made up for her "terrible mistake" by staying at the hospital and caring for Troy on a 24-hour basis. She had even taken a leave of absence from her job in order to make sure she was present any time he needed dialysis, cracked an eyelid open or took a shit. She was more of a slave to his ridiculous demands now than she was when he was whipping her ass every day. I could hear him in the background whenever I talked to her on the phone.

"Fluff my pillow, this water ain't cold, tell the nurse to bring me a fresh pitcher with some ice, empty my pee can, go to McDonald's and get me some real food." His commands were relentless. I wondered if Myeisha had ever considered how things would be if she had added just a few more pinches of White Oleander to Troy's coffee. I know I did.

"They said Troy is ready to be released now, so I need you to come to the hospital," Myeisha stated, sounding on edge. I could hear Troy in the background giving the nurse a hard time about taking his medicine.

"Well, that's good that he's getting out, but I don't see what that has to do with me. You know you my girl and I'd love to help you, but it's Saturday evening and I'm relaxing. The last thing I need is Troy fucking up my mood."

"I know Troy isn't perfect. I've already told him that things had to change between us. But right now, he needs someone to help take care of him," Myeisha said, sounding like she trying to convince herself more than she was trying to convince me.

"To each their own, but I'd drop him off right at his mother's house and let her deal with him. Sick or not, he won't step foot in my house ever again."

Bret rolled over in his sleep and rubbed his foot along my calf, releasing butterflies in my stomach.

"Look Myeisha, I have to go. I'm glad Troy is doing better, but that doesn't change how I feel about him, so I'm not coming to the hospital," I stated firmly.

"I'm not asking you to come to the hospital for Troy, I'm asking you to come because Dr. Monroe wants to talk to you."

"About what!" I exclaimed, now on full alert.

"I don't know. He wouldn't say. I'm really scared, Gen. What if they figured everything out?" I could tell she had stepped into the hallway away from Troy because I couldn't hear him nagging the nurse anymore.

"If they figured everything out, then the police would be asking to speak to me, *not* Dr. Monroe."

As sensible as my explanation sounded, I was just as nervous as Myeisha. Why would Dr. Monroe want to talk to me before releasing Troy? I wasn't his relative, much less his friend. If he had care instructions to go over, then he would do that with Myeisha. I couldn't think of a reason why he would want to see me and that made me very uneasy.

"Okay, I'll come down, but if anyone asks you anything before I get there, don't say a word.

She agreed and I left the warmness of Bret's body and the coolness of silk sheets to face whatever obstacle lay ahead for me at County General Hospital.

Chapter 32

County General was packed. It wasn't flu season, but there was apparently some type of bug in the air. Ailing, impatient people filled the chairs and stood impatiently in line in the emergency room lobby. I made a bee-line through the crowd of chaos to the elevators. I flinched and pulled the neck of my shirt up around my mouth as a barrier when an old, sickly looking man sneezed on me in the elevator. Another lady in the elevator was holding the hand of the cutest, freckled-faced, redhead little boy I had ever seen. Despite his sunken eyes and snotty nose, he was as adorable as the brown teddy bear he was clutching in his left hand. When the little boy went into a fit of coughs, his mother picked him up and lovingly patted his back as he lay on her shoulder. I would never know what type of mother I would have been if Jayson and I would have conceived a child together. Although it hurt my heart to know he had chosen someone else to start a family with, it was for the best that we didn't bring a child into this mess. I knew, firsthand, how difficult it was to not have a father around growing up. Even though it wasn't my father's fault, I still resented not having him there for my graduation, for my wedding and all the other important moments a girl wants to share with her father.

The elevator opened and I quickly exited the small space into the corridor. I released my makeshift mask and headed to Troy's room. I had barely taken three steps towards my destination when someone tapped me on the shoulder from behind. I turned to see Dr. Monroe standing there, dressed in a pair of sky blue scrubs.

"I'm glad I caught you," he said, smiling and showing his perfectly straight, ivory teeth. "I'm getting ready to head into surgery, so unfortunately I only have a few minutes to spare. There's something that I need to discuss with you urgently. If you don't mind, I think we should discuss this matter in private. My office is just around the corner."

Not waiting for a response, he turned around and led me to a room less than ten feet from where we were standing.

"That's the perk when you're the Chief Surgeon and Head of Internal Medicine: you get your own office," he laughed, pushing opening the door to the office, then closing it softly behind me.

"Have a seat," he said, motioning toward a brown leather chair on the other side of his desk that he was now seated at.

I looked around the room, taking in the décor. Everything was modern and artsy, with dark woods and leather with punches of red in the rug and window covering. Several impressionist paintings hung on the wall next to a bookshelf filled with medical books, awards and a couple of pictures of men who I assumed where his colleagues or friends. It was obvious, from his lush quarters at the hospital, that he was very important and well-respected at County General. I sat down reluctantly. I still felt uneasy about not knowing what exactly he wanted to discuss with me.

"Troy is a very lucky man," Dr. Monroe began. I nodded in agreement, but made sure to keep my face expressionless. "I've treated a lot of people and it's unsettling when you have patients that are fighting for their life or are on their death bed with no family, friends or loved ones who care enough about them to be there. I admire Myeisha's commitment to him as a partner. She's been here every day taking care of him."

"Myeisha is a caring person. She doesn't have an evil bone in her body. She would do the same for me or any of her family members or friends in the same situation," I said, hoping I didn't sound too defensive.

"Yes, she seems like a lovely person. I don't know if I can say the same about Troy. I hate to pass judgment, but I think she can do a lot better. He's been driving my staff crazy, which is why I decided to release him early. I wouldn't do it if he weren't medically stable to, but he's made a quick turn-around and is doing much better sooner than I expected."

"I trust that you will do whatever is medically responsible, but did you really ask to speak to me to discuss Myeisha and Troy's relationship?" I asked, getting straight to the point.

Dr. Monroe blushed. His cheeks turned a deep pink and he nervously ran his fingers through his blonde hair. Even embarrassed, Dr. Monroe was one fine-ass white man. The fact that he probably made more money than I could figure out how to spend was just as attractive.

"I apologize, Genevieve, if I've compromised your integrity in any way. I really should've found another way to go about things. I won't waste another minute of your time. The nurse is just going over a few last minute instructions with your friends. You can join them in the Troy's room," Dr. Monroe said, pushing away from the desk.

"With all due respect, Dr. Monroe, you brought me here with the intention to discuss something with me that you obviously thought was very important and I don't intend to leave this room until you tell me what that was."

I couldn't believe that I was talking to him so boldly, but I felt that I had nothing to lose. If he knew something about what happened to Troy, I wasn't going to go home and walk on eggshells, expecting the police to bust down my door at any moment. I'd rather deal with it sooner than later.

"Okay..." he said, tapping a silver pen against the edge of his desk. Whatever he had to say was making him more nervous than I was. "Like I was saying earlier, it really is beautiful when... umm... two people care for each other. I was wondering, do you have someone special in your life?" he finally spat out.

I was relieved to hear that I wasn't a suspected attempted murderer. I looked down at my hand and realized that my ring finger was naked. I had gotten into the habit of removing my wedding ring around Bret. It was part of the illusion that I created when I was around him - that I was his and only his. Of course, we both knew darn well that it wasn't true, but Bret told me his dick would go limp at any reminder that I was Jayson's wife. The other day, he told me he couldn't wait until me and Jayson were divorced so he didn't have to pretend anymore. Today and the only other time I had seen Dr. Monroe, I had forgotten to put my ring back on, therefore, he had probably concluded that I was single and ready to mingle. The urge to tell him that I was as free and up for grabs was compelling. He was a hell of a catch - sexy, intelligent, gorgeous and prestigious. What more could a woman ask for in a man? I decided, for once, to tell the truth since lying had come with some serious consequences lately. Besides, juggling two men was enough; I couldn't keep up with a third. Fifteen minutes later, I had told Dr. Monroe everything about my relationship with Jayson. Yes, I was married, but to a man that had chosen to have another wife and child. Yes, I was married, but I had not slept with my husband in months and didn't plan on doing so. Yes, I was married, but not for long. When I got done telling him my story, I was scared I had run him off. Why would a man with so much responsibility and so much going for him already want to deal with such non-sense?

Paging Dr. Monroe to OR... Paging Dr. Monroe to OR.

The intercom system blared through the hospital hallway and penetrated the office door. Dr. Monroe ignored page and continued talking without pause.

"Your husband doesn't deserve you. He should go to jail for what he did. I promise I won't ever treat you that way," Dr. Monroe stated passionately, his eyes full of promise. I knew right then it was the beginning of a beautiful thing.

Chapter 33

With a million dollars in the bank and the money that I was slowly transferring over from Jayson's account my safety nest was growing. Pretty soon, I would be able to file for a divorce from Jayson and stop screwing around with Bret. I already had what I needed from both of them, so their time was up. Things were going great between me and Dr. Monroe or, Teddy, as I now affectionately called him. He wasn't needy like Bret or selfish and stuck on himself like Jayson. He liked to go boating on his days off, was great at cooking French cuisine and even spoke the language. Teddy was down to earth, easy to talk to, pleasing on the eyes and we got along great. As we grew closer and closer, Jayson and Bret became more of a nuisance to me. Since I wanted to fight for the house and alimony, I had to deal with Jayson a little longer, but there was no more reason for me to deal with Bret. He had already taken care of the issue with the marriage records for me, so there was not any good reason that I could think of to keep this charade up for any longer. I could care less if he told Jayson that we had been having an affair. Jayson had a wife and a kid, so there wasn't anything he could criticize me about. He'd have some damn nerve to get mad about my affair when he was a practicing polygamist. If Bret let the cat out of the bag, that only meant that there was one less skeleton in my closet I had to deal with. It would be refreshing to stop playing games with Jayson and lay everything out on the table.

It was Friday night and Jayson was gone again.

"Sorry, I have another big case. I might not make it in by midnight," Jayson had said when he had called me from his cell phone an hour ago. I pretended to believe.

"Okay, honey, see you then," I said, rolling my eyes up at the ceiling. As soon as he hung up, I grabbed my purse and keys and headed out the door. Tonight was the night I would end things with Bret. I simply did not have a need, desire or reason for him any longer.

The dark sky, howling winds and scattered showers warned me of an approaching storm. I grabbed an umbrella from the coat closet on the way out the door. I had to hop on the interstate to reach Bret's house on the east side of town. I hated driving the freeway when it was raining. Slippery streets, bad judgment, and high speeds were the sure makings for an accident. If I was lucky, maybe I could make it to Bret's before it started pouring. I couldn't wait any longer to end things with him. If things went smoothly, I could be back home in bed, eating ice cream and talking to Teddy on the phone in less than a couple of hours. As soon as I opened the door to leave, a flash of lightning cut through the clouds off in the distance. There was definitely a storm brewing and if I would have known exactly how treacherous it was, I would have stayed home that night.

Chapter 34

"What are you doing here?" Bret said through the crack of his front door. Not only was his tone of voice rude, but it was so unlike Bret to not be excited to see me, even if I did arrive uninvited.

"Let me in. It's raining cats and dogs out here!" I exclaimed. My purple umbrella was taking a beating from the relentless downpour of rain.

"You shouldn't have come unannounced. I have company… you'll have to come back later," Bret stated roughly while peering at me through the crack. His usual calm, sea blue eyes were menacing. His words came out seething through gritted teeth, but he wasn't yelling. His voice remained just above a whisper. Whoever was there, he didn't want them to hear what was going on.

"Look Bret, I don't care about your little bimbo or whoever you have over. I just wanted to get something off of my chest and I felt it was best if I said what I had to say to you in person. I don't have to come in if you don't want me to, even though it would be nice if you let me come into the foyer just to get out of this weather."

Although I felt a slight twinge of jealousy that Bret had moved on so quickly, it only meant that he would take my dumping him with a grain of salt. Bret continued to glare at me through the slit, but refused to budge.

"Okay, if it's like that, then I'll just say what I have to say right now," I started.

"Bret, where are you? Are you coming back to bed?" a male's voice called out.

My head started to swim and the oyster soup and crackers I had for dinner threatened to come back up. The churning in my stomach initiated a wave of vibrations that traveled through my body until I stood on Bret's stoop, shaking so violently that it probably looked like I was going into convulsions. I was drenched, freezing cold and had just heard something that would make the hair on any woman's neck stand up. It wasn't just that I heard a man's voice asking Bret when he was coming back to bed, but the voice I heard was without a doubt, Jayson's.

Bret tried to close the door as quickly as possible, but it was too late. My "woman scorned" reflexes were much quicker and superior to his. With one sturdy shove, the door flew open with a loud smacking sound from the impact it made with Bret's forehead. He recovered swiftly and tried to block my descent down the hallway to his bedroom. He held one hand up to the swelling lump on his head and the other hand against the wall in an attempt to block my path. He was still dazed from the blow of the solid wood door against his head, so it was fairly easy to push past him.

Jayson pulled the covers over his head, like a child hiding from the boogeyman, as soon as he saw me enter the room. I snatched the white sheets from him and pummeled him with my fists as hard as I could. It didn't matter which body part I made contact with because I was not concerned about causing him injury. I wanted to hurt him just as badly as he had just hurt me. I screamed murderous threats at the top of my lungs.

"I'll kill you, fucking dirty motherfucker! How dare you do this to me?" I hollered, slamming my fists into him harder and harder with each threat until I was slobbering like a mad dog and completely out of breath.

I lay in a sweaty heap on the floor at the end of the bed, my eyes closed and my head in my lap. I could sense Bret watching from the doorway, too afraid to enter. I could hear Jayson get out of the bed and shuffle across the room to the bathroom. Then, I heard the click as he locked the door.

Go hide, just like a little bitch, I thought to myself.

When I first realized that it was my husband's voice coming from Bret's room, I was too stunned to understand what it really meant. The anger and madness had taken over too quickly to get any further than comprehending that my husband was apparently a homosexual. But suddenly, the reality that our relationship was built on a lie from the very beginning dawned on me. I could accept the fact that Jayson had another wife. Maybe he was a man torn between two beautiful women, so he decided to have his cake and eat it too. There probably isn't a man alive who wouldn't do the same thing if he thought he could get away with it. But to know that he was equally, if not more, attracted to men than women was a harsher reality to face.

The room was silent, excluding the pitter-patter of rain against the windowpane. As much as I despised Jasmine for being the first wife, I couldn't help but think how this would affect her and her child. I'm sure she had no idea that her husband preferred dick just as much as she did.

"How long has this been going on?" I asked. I wasn't sure if I was thinking out loud or if I really even wanted to know the answer.

"I think it would be in your best interest to leave or I'll be forced to call the police," Bret responded.

"I'm not talking to you. I'm talking to Jayson," I said, standing up and walking over to the locked bathroom door.

There was complete silence on the other end. Bret left the room. I didn't know if he was leaving to call the police or not and I didn't care. I wanted some answers from Jayson before I left.

"You owe me some answers," I cried. Still more silence.

"I swear, Gen. It's only been going on for about a month," Jayson confessed.

"But you've been gay forever, right?" I asked sarcastically.

"I guess I've always had some sort of attraction to men, but I've never been with a man until now. I know you won't believe me, but tonight was the first time that I've… umm… ever you know… been with a man before."

He was right, I didn't believe him, but I hoped, for my sake, he was telling the truth.

"First, I find out that you have another wife and a child and now, I find out that you're gay!"

"What do you mean? I don't have another wife or a child," Jayson said.

"Come on, Jayson. You can stop with all the lies now."

"I promise you, Gen, I don't know what you're talking about."

"So, you're saying you don't know who Jasmine is? Are you so evil and sick that you would sit here and even deny that you have a child named Jewel?"

"Yes. That's exactly what I'm telling you. Look, I'm as busted as busted gets, so if I had anything more to confess, I would assume now would be the perfect time, but I am telling you I do not have another wife or a child."

I was about to argue my point and bring up the marriage license and the judge he had bribed to cover up for him until I realized I had never seen any of the evidence firsthand. Bret told me he saw the marriage license and that he had spoken to the judge, but I had received all my information through Bret. When I had asked Bret for her address, he had refused to give it to me and a records search had yielded no results. I had decided Bret was right in suggesting I not confront Jasmine and had feared of involving an innocent child in our mess. The only thing I had ever seen for myself was Jayson at the restaurant with Jasmine, but I had never spoken to her personally.

"Well, if Jasmine doesn't exist, why did I see you out on a date with her at Geisha? I saw you and her there together with my own eyes."

"I went to Geisha with a client of mine. I admit things were starting to get out of hand with her. She was constantly hitting on me and I admit I was inappropriate at times, too. She was a long-term client and she asked me to dinner to celebrate a year of me representing her as a client. After that night, I asked Bret to take her on as his client since things were getting out of hand, but her name is Clara, not Jasmine, and I'm not married to her and I do not have a child with her."

Something told me that Jayson was telling the truth. Had Bret played off my fear that Jayson was cheating by making up the story about another wife and another child. Now, I was positive that he had asked me out to dinner at Geisha only because he knew Jayson would be there with his client. He knew I was paranoid and would jump to conclusions. He had taken the rift between me and Jayson and made it into a huge gap. Bret had pulled the wool over both of our eyes to get what he really wanted... my husband.

Chapter 35

Myeisha was too busy caring for Troy to be as supportive as I needed her to be.

"What the fuck, Gen! Are you telling me that Jayson is a butt pirate?"

"I guess if that's what you want to call it," I said into the receiver.

I could hear Troy in the background, bitching and complaining, as usual, and I couldn't handle hearing his voice under the circumstances. It was days like this that I wished Myeisha would have slipped one more spoonful of Mama Rose's secret stash into his coffee.

"I'll let you go, Myeisha. It sounds like you have your hands full."

"Nothing is more important than my girl. Troy can wait," Myeisha said.

I could hear Troy responding to Myeisha's comment. His voice was muffled, but I could make out the words "bitch" and "shit" very clearly.

"Call me back tonight. Maybe we could go out for drinks after you put your dog down for bed," I said sarcastically.

"Okay, sounds like a plan. I'll call you later around eight," Myeisha promised before hanging up.

I desperately needed to talk to someone about what had happened last night.

My sister was the only one I could talk to since Mama Rose would undoubtedly follow through with my threat to kill Jayson if she ever found out the truth. She picked up on the first ring and listened intently as I spilled my guts about Bret and Jayson.

"I guess I can see why he was confused about his sexuality. I was too before I came out. You're torn between your feelings and what society tells you is right or wrong. When I finally came out, I had so-called friends who just stopped talking to me. Even Mama Rose made it clear that although I was still her child, she would never accept my choices. She's fine as long as I don't bring up my sexuality or bring any of my partners around her. That's why I chose to avoid her altogether for the most part. But regardless if Jayson was confused, he should have been truthful to you and he should have never committed to you if he was unsure."

I could always count on Georgette to be rational and see both sides of the story.

"I agree with you Georgette, but at the same time, I can't help but wonder if Mama Rose is right. Are all men sex-crazed, untrustworthy, low-life scum?"

"Take my advice, Gen. Don't listen to nothing Mama Rose says. If you do, you'll end up lonely, miserable and black-hearted, just like she is."

I thought about Dr. Monroe. He didn't seem sex-crazed or untrustworthy. I wasn't going to risk a chance at a good relationship with him over mistakes another man made.

"You're right. I would say *most,* but not *all* men are untrustworthy," I said. "Maybe if our father hadn't done Mama Rose wrong, she wouldn't feel that way."

"You need to stop listening to those lies Mama Rose fed you about our father. He was a good man. Sure, he flirted with the women folk every now and then, but he didn't deserve what Mama Rose did to him in the end," Georgette fussed.

"Mama Rose took care of Daddy until the very end, as far as I can remember," I stated defensively.

"That's exactly the issue. What you remember isn't much because you were still so young at the time, but I remember everything. Daddy's heart got weak when he was still young. It was a heart murmur issue he was born with, but unlike most folks who grow out of it as they get older, his got worse. Mama Rose had suspected him of cheating right before he took ill, so when he was bed-ridden, she made sure to let him understand how indebted he was to her. Sometimes, she even made him beg her to change his bed pan or fix his favorite meal. Pretty soon, I took over taking care of Daddy the majority of the time. He would turn his head away from her and stare at the wall when she walked in the room. All she would do for him after a while is make his tea and she wouldn't even do that right because he always complained that it was too sweet. When he passed, she had a thrown together funeral at some church that we didn't even attend and said Daddy wanted it that way, but I knew she wasn't telling the truth."

I had never heard such anger in Georgette's voice. I recalled Mama Rose's advice when she handed me the small brown pouch.

Put a couple of pinches of this in his tea or coffee every morning. Make sure to add a couple of teaspoons of sugar to cover up the bitterness.

Could Mama Rose have poisoned my father? I knew it was a question that I would never know the answer to. After all, I could no longer deny that Mama Rose and I were alike in some ways; we were both willing to take to our secrets to the grave.

Sequel coming soon!!